In the sparks of chaos, steel hearts are tested.

LEGENDS OF THE ROADS
BORN TO BE WILD
IRON CITY KNIGHTS
SUPERIOR PERFORMANCE
LEGENDARY RIDERS

FORGE
ML NYSTROM

LEGENDS OF THE ROADS
BORN TO BE WILD
IRON CITY KNIGHTS
SUPERIOR PERFORMANCE
LEGENDARY RIDERS

FORGE

ML NYSTROM

HOT TREE PUBLISHING

Forge © 2026 by ML Nostrum

All rights reserved. No part of this book may be used or reproduced in any written, electronic, recorded, or photocopied format without the express permission from the author or publisher as allowed under the terms and conditions with which it was purchased or as strictly permitted by applicable copyright law. Any unauthorized distribution, circulation or use of this text may be a direct infringement of the author's rights, and those responsible may be liable in law accordingly. Thank you for respecting the work of this author.

Forge is a work of fiction. All names, characters, events and places found therein are either from the author's imagination or used fictitiously. Any similarity to persons alive or dead, actual events, locations, or organizations is entirely coincidental and not intended by the author.

For information, contact the publisher, Hot Tree Publishing.

www.hottreepublishing.com

Editing: Hot Tree Editing

Cover Designer: BookSmith Design

E-book ISBN: 978-1-923252-60-8

Paperback ISBN: 978-1-923252-61-5

To Stephanie Cox and Amanda Ramey,
Two ladies who inspired me to write this story.
Y'all rock!

1

The distant roar of a motorcycle hit Camshaft's ear. He identified the rumble as a classic Harley cruiser that needed a timing update. The sound wasn't unusual around this Pittsburgh neighborhood, since this was the area where the Iron City Knights MC kept their two businesses and clubhouse, such as it was. One was the machine shop and forge, mostly owned and run by Quillon, a senior member and the current vice president. The other was a titty bar where the members met and hung out. Cam worked for both.

The noise got closer and slower. Only a few members owned Harleys, and Cam briefly wondered who it was, but as the sound faded in and out, he put it out of his mind. He glanced at his watch as he stood outside the strip joint, the crisp air burning his nose as he took in the late-fall twilight. His break from working security for the place was almost over, but no one worried about a time clock. It was a typical Thursday night, although not many patrons graced the stools surrounding the stage. No drama, which was nice for a change.

After the past few months, some easy, boring nights were just the ticket.

A rival club, the Slaggers MC, had tried to move into the neighborhood, bringing drugs and racketeering to the local businesses. The Knights had to deal with that, along with the internal struggles of restructuring. Ultimately, the club elected a new president, Wolf, and the Knights pushed out the bad guys.

He was afraid this might be the calm before the storm.

The distant motorcycle wasn't so distant anymore. A big red machine cruised down the street, one Cam had never seen before. The distinctive *potato-potato-potato* sound came to his ears as *poTA—to-poTA—to*. He frowned at the uneven chugging. None of the Knights had a bike that color, nor would they let the timing of the V-twin engine get that far off. New rider, but of what kind? Friend or foe?

He put his hand to the gun he now carried on his hip and held his breath as the vehicle slowed down and parked on the street in front of the club. The Slaggers had done a drive-by here some months ago. No one got hurt, and the Knights wanted to keep it that way. They'd ramped up their vigilance, and for now, everyone carried a gun except for Wolf.

The person who dismounted from the bike wore black riding chaps and a red leather riding jacket with black gloves and boots. The full-face helmet sported an open-mouthed lizard demon theme. Cam's frown deepened. No one he knew would be caught dead in such a getup. This guy was either a wannabe biker or some college kid with more money than sense.

A moment later, Cam's curiosity piqued as two thick blonde braids appeared when the rider took off the artsy headgear. Icy blue eyes met his in a direct stare as the woman secured her vehicle and confidently strode up to him.

"I'm looking for Walter Arborough. Is he in there?"

Cam jolted at the smooth Southern alto. "Uh… who?"

The woman rolled her eyes, then cocked out a hip and crossed her arms. "Waaaalllteeer Arrrrbor-rrroooooough." She drew out the name as if he would recognize it any better if she said it slower. "Is he in there?"

His irritation flared up. "I don't know any Walter, period."

She huffed. "I'm told he hangs out here all the time."

Cam crossed his own arms and stood his ground. "Well, sweetheart, it doesn't matter if he's in there or not. It's a private club. You can't go in."

She gave him a saccharin smile. "Well, darlin', I've spent the last two days driving my van up from Sarasota, Florida, dragging my bike and other gear in a rickety trailer to find him. It's sitting over at Planet Fitness while I finish this long-ass journey. That's around eleven hundred miles and roughly twenty hours. I'm sick of being on the road and dealing with stupid drivers who either don't know what a turn signal is or poke along in the left passing lane for miles. I'm tired, and I'm cranky as hell. Therefore, I don't think you're gonna stop me." She moved around him to the plain front door and opened it.

"Yo, I said you can't go in there!" Cam shouted as

the woman barged straight into the club. She was right. Unless he put his hands on her and *made* her stay out, he was helpless.

The few patrons around the stage were more interested in drinking than paying attention to the dancer. Though to be fair, Ellie wasn't putting a lot of effort into her performance. So when the blonde woman burst into the bar, all eyes targeted her.

"Walter Arborough. Is he in here somewhere?"

Cam jumped at the authoritative yell. This woman wasn't messing around.

Melter leered as he took in her leather boots and riding attire. "You want an audition, baby?"

The blonde huffed and rolled her eyes.

Cam tried to stop her once more. "Look, lady, this is a private club. I don't know any Walter—"

"He's the owner, from what I understand."

He blinked. "You mean Scrap?"

She flipped an impatient hand at him. "Whatever. I'm here to meet the owner of the bar. He's supposed to be the president of the Iron City Knights, so someone here has to know him. You gonna find him for me, or do I need to keep hollering until he shows up?"

Cam's inner alarm bells started ringing. Something told him he was going to regret his next action, but like a mudslide rolling down a hill, there was no stopping this. He pointed to the back of the room, where Scrap and Baghouse were engaged in a game of chess.

The woman squared her shoulders and then seemed to hesitate, taking several deep breaths through her nose and blowing out through her full lips. It pissed Cam off, as she was so gung ho to get into the club but now had gone cold in her quest.

"That's him? The president?"

Cam nodded. "Ex-president, but yeah, that's him."

She shook herself before dropping her self-confident mask back into place. Her steps were sure and steady as she clomped across the wood floor toward the two men, stopping right next to their table.

"Are you Walter Arborough?"

Scrap scowled at the interruption to his game. He raised his head from the board at a sharp angle, partially hiding the black patch that covered his empty socket. He stared at the woman with his one good eye.

Both of them glared at each other like snarling dogs, and Cam's stomach dropped. A sense of foreboding hit his gut as he noted that the woman's shocking blue eyes matched Scrap's single iris.

"Who the fuck are you?" Scrap sneered with such contempt, Cam thought the woman might burn from the acid.

But she spat back with just as much ire as Scrap. "I'm your fuckin' daughter. That's who, asshole!"

2

Cam pulled a glowing red spike from the furnace with long, thick tongs and laid it on the anvil. The bandana across his forehead had already soaked up as much as it would, and sweat dripped down his face from the heat. He'd knocked off early from the machine shop so he could make a few blades. Knife-making was a hobby he loved that helped him de-stress and also earn some extra money.

He reached for the heaviest cross-peen hammer and started pounding and shaping the hot metal. The crack of the hammer hitting the spike filled the empty forge, sparks flying freely in the air as he drew out the shape, making it long and flat. He picked up the half-formed blade and placed it back in the roaring furnace. He would repeat this process several times before he was ready for the grinder.

Cam stretched the stiff, sore muscles of his shoulders. He'd spent the day turning some custom fixed axles on the shop lathes for several classic cars, which included forcing on the bearings. His back protested that job already. Coupled with swinging a hammer for an hour, he was hurting.

The tendons in his lower back complained as he put the metal into the furnace to reheat once again. The forge had a pneumatic power hammer, but the compressor had to be replaced. Those suckers were expensive, so better to maintain it than to buy a new machine. Someday, he wanted to own and operate his own forge, but that was a long way off. For now, he had to work any metal manually until Quillon fixed the hammer.

Suddenly, his back seized up, and he cursed the cramping muscle. The last time he went to a doctor, he got a prescription for muscle relaxers and anti-inflammatories, but they didn't help with the chronic issue. He was out of the medication anyway.

Melter will have something, he thought as he hobbled over to sit on one of the shop stools and relieve the pressure. The man always seemed to have a supply of pot and pills, although he wasn't a dealer.

At least he said he wasn't. No one knew for sure, but if someone in the club wanted fennies or oxys, Melter usually had them.

Cam's thoughts reverted to the events of last night, and he wondered what had happened to the woman who'd barged into the club and announced she was Scrap's long-lost daughter. The old man had actually been speechless for a moment before exploding in the biggest fit of anger anyone in the club had ever seen. That was impressive, given Scrap's reputation for a permanent bad temper. The woman hadn't backed down an inch, though, and both of them proceeded to yell and curse at each other.

"I don't have a gawddamn daughter!"

"Ya damn well might. Raquel told me she wasn't sure. My dad told me about you and said he wasn't sure either."

"That fucking jagoff can go piss up a rope!"

"He's dead, asshole."

"Good!"

Cam had listened to a few stories about Scrap's old lady. No one talked about it much, as any mention of Raquel's name would send Scrap into a cursing frenzy. From what Cam understood, the woman cheated on him with regularity and finally ran off with some man she met on the internet. Rumor had it that she ended up in Florida, but no one knew for sure.

Shortly after Raquel took off, Scrap had the accident at the steel plant that left him with half a hand, one eye, and a myriad of scars all over his body. He used the settlement from that accident to buy the titty bar and invest in the machine shop. Raquel's name became forbidden, and Scrap had soured on women in general.

It didn't make a lot of sense to Cam. Scrap spent every day in a club looking at topless women he had no interest in and didn't like. Perhaps it was proximity to the strippers that eventually numbed whoever worked there. Cam himself thought it was really cool when he was a prospect that he got to see naked women all the time, but now, after so many years of working security at Attic, he was kind of over it too.

Cam slowly leaned over to snag a bottle of cold water from the mini fridge under a workbench. He drained half of it as his back spasm finally started to let go, still thinking about last night. The woman was definitely a surprise, and he could see the family resemblance. Cute, feisty, and built like a brick house. She wasn't a little woman, but not a big one either. Lots of rounded curves and a nice-sized rear end with the perfect shape to fill a man's hands. He wondered what her name was.

"Listen, jackass. Do me a favor and take a DNA test. If it's false, I'll take my happy ass and leave. If it's true, I'll still take my happy ass and leave, but I'll have the answers I need."

"Fuck off and get lost!"

Cam frowned as he drained the rest of the water from the bottle, letting his cheeks bulge out. He wasn't above confronting a woman about bad behavior; it happened at Attic more than once when a dancer got mouthy or broke the house rules. But cursing at your daughter—or potential daughter—wasn't something he agreed with, especially when one simple test would put the question to bed. A cheek swab that took less than three seconds and a week to get lab results. Quick and easy.

The problem? Scrap's legendary stubbornness. The man could drive a saint to murder.

Cam bent over slowly, his back painfully protesting. *I oughta ask Melter for some painkillers later tonight.* Fridays were generally more exciting than Thursdays, but hopefully, it would be a peaceful night and he could relax a bit.

Sabrina lowered the weight stack with an easy movement, catching her breath before rising from the machine and wiping it down. Planet Fitness was her go-to place for several reasons: the membership fee was reasonable, she could go to any facility in the country, and it had 24/7 access to showers. That was a big deal to her now, since she was essentially homeless.

She picked up her sweat towel and made her way to the locker room. It was early Friday afternoon, and she was no closer to her goal than she had been when she arrived in Pittsburgh.

Answers. Not that hard of an ask, was it? She just wanted some answers, and then she could walk away to live her life. Walter or Scrap or whatever he called himself could live his, and neither of them would have to speak to or see the other again. She wasn't looking for a father figure or long-lost daddy to hug her and tell her how much he loved her. She didn't need that shit. What she needed was closure.

Yeah, that's it. Closure, she thought as the water beat down on her head from the shower. Her plastic caddy of toiletries sat next to her flip-flop-clad feet. This was nothing new to her. When she was little, her father drove a truck, and very often they spent the night in the sleeper cab at a Love's, Pilot, or Flying J stop. The facilities at those chains were usually pretty nice, but Ernie insisted on her wearing the cheap footwear anyway, as toe fungus was still a thing in public showers, no matter how clean they seemed.

Ernie. Dad.

Sabrina's eyes teared up as she shut off the water and pulled her towel from the hook outside the stall. She bent over and vigorously dried her hair before flinging it behind her and wrapping her body in the thick cloth. The man who raised her after her mom split had been an anchor throughout her life. Raquel was a vague figure who showed up once or twice a year to ask for money and make remarks about how big her daughter had grown. Sometimes she stayed for a few weeks, long enough to get Sabrina's hopes up, but inevitably Raquel simply picked up and left. No notice, no calls. Just an empty closet and taking whatever money she could find or stuff she could pawn in the house. It surprised Sabrina that Ernie put up with it, but for some reason, he did. But she remembered the anger every time she saw her dad's disappointed, hurt face after Raquel left again.

Sabrina had no fucks to give about her mother.

She supposed that some women just didn't have any maternal instincts even though they could still birth children. No, it was her dad who she'd depended on until the day he died. It didn't have to happen, which made it worse. A road-raging asshole lost his temper and cut off the big rig Ernie was driving on a long haul. The dashcam showed the dumbass brake-checking the semi on a highway full of fast-moving traffic. Such a *stupid* move! At that speed, the sporty Camaro was toast when Ernie plowed into the back as they crossed an overpass. Then that car hit another one and started a massive pileup of vehicles that had no time to stop and no room to swerve out of the way. Ernie's hard-right veer to minimize the crash caused the accident footage to appear twisted. The rig skidded and flipped onto its side, breaking through the safety rails and plunging over to the road below. Ernie survived the accident itself, but his injuries were too severe. He died three days later, only regaining consciousness once to say goodbye and tell her to find Walter Arborough.

The asshole who caused the accident? Manslaughter and a slew of other charges landed him in jail for the foreseeable future. The sentence was ten years before parole would be on the table.

She hoped he rotted.

Sabrina swiped at the foggy mirror and shook herself from the memories of those final days. If her dad were still alive, she'd be happy and content back in Sarasota, taking care of the house and working for her friend Amelia. Instead, her life had taken an entirely different direction, and she had no idea what her future looked like now.

Hell, she didn't even know who she was anymore.

"That's why you're here, dummy," she whispered to the watery image.

She combed through the wet strands, then used the provided blow-dryer to dry her thick honey-gold mane. Ernie's Latino heritage showed in his dark brown eyes and brown hair when he was young. Later in life, he was bald as a cue ball with a faint ring of gray over his ears. His family all looked alike, except for her. Everyone just assumed Sabrina favored her estranged mother, as Raquel had light brown hair and blue eyes. Even so, at an early age, Sabrina learned to say "recessive genes" when people looked at her odd coloring.

"Enough," she admonished herself. Thankfully, no one was in the locker room with her.

Last night, she'd confronted the man who might be her bio-father, and he'd thrown a shit fit before turning her away. Tonight, she would try again. Today, she needed to find work.

Her van and trailer were parked in two spots at the back of the lot. Someone had converted the Ford Transit into a cool little home space before she tapped into her savings and bought it. It had a small living area across from a kitchenette, solar panels on top for electricity, and a double bed in back with storage underneath, but there was no bathroom, thus she needed her gym membership. The small box trailer held her motorcycle and a few other items.

This was all she had in the world. No obligations. No tangibles. No relations.

It was cool, but at the same time, it kinda sucked.

The fall weather was way cooler here than in Sarasota, and she shivered as she climbed into the back of the van and shut the door. The small space heater kicked on, toasting up the air.

"Hey, guys," Sabrina greeted her pets as she pulled out the mini single-cup Keurig and set it on the counter.

A large vertical cage sat just behind the driver's seat. The two bearded dragons pushed at each other, trying to climb the dried tree branch in the center of the multilevel home. One was heading for the heating rock, the other pushing at the door.

"Settle down, Rugrat. I'll let you out in a minute."

Coffee in hand and the reptile securely hanging on her shoulder, Sabrina pulled out her phone and stuck a Bluetooth bud in her ear to call her friend.

"Yo, whassup!" Amelia answered. "Gettin' sick of the north country?"

Sabrina leaned back on the built-in couch cushions. "I ain't worn out my welcome yet, if that's what you want to know."

"Didja find him?"

Sabrina sighed and reached out a finger to pet Rugrat's rough head. "Yeah, I did. Bastard won't take the DNA test, though."

"You'll just have to turn on that Southern charm of yours. Battin' your eyes and shit like that."

Sabrina laughed. "Since when have I ever been sugar-sweet?"

"You oughta try it sometime. Might get you some better results."

"Whatever. Hey, do you have a work connection up here?"

Amelia paused, and Sabrina imagined her friend was scrolling through her contacts. "Possibly. My girl Joelle used to be up there. I'll check with her to see if she has any connections. She owes me a favor anyway. You need money?"

"The well ain't dry yet, but I can see the bottom."

Amelia giggled. "No problem, darlin'. I'll shoot you a message with whatever I find out and get Joelle to make the intros. She'll hook you up."

"Thanks, babe. You're a real peach."

Amelia's laughter tinkled in her ear. "That's what they all say until they get to the pit. Take care, precious."

Sabrina ended the call, then sniffled and put a hand to her forehead. If she stopped to think about all that had happened to her in recent months, she would lose it completely and never make it out of the van that was her one and only safe haven.

Nope, I ain't got time to waste. Gotta keep moving and get stuff done.

She tapped Rugrat under his chin. "Mama's got a lot to do today. Wish me luck."

3

Cam eyed the group of men who sat at the edge of the stage. A bachelor party was the last thing he wanted to deal with this evening, but the group was already there and half drunk when he arrived for work. They'd spent a huge amount of money on booze and boobs and were now fully drunk and getting louder. One man wore a sash, declaring himself to be the groom.

"I gadda see ash many tits ash I can tonide. I'm gettin' married tomorrow, an' I can only see one set for the rest of mah life!"

Ellie complied by giving the man a special shimmy, and he stared at the jiggling double Ds as if he'd never seen boobs before. Cam wondered what the man's capacity was before he got sick.

"Crazy night, yeah?"

Cam turned to see his best friend and current president of the club, Wolf, had joined him. A long streak of gray that started at his forehead bisected the man's midnight mane. "I guess so. Just those guys over there having fun before doomsday tomorrow."

Wolf chuckled. "Married life isn't so bad. Quillon is happy as shit."

"You're not married yet."

Wolf's massive shoulder lifted in a shrug. "Semantics. I'm popping the question to Jazz after the house is built. The insurance finally came through, and the slab got poured last week. Winter construction is gonna be slow, but we're pretty content for now."

Cam clicked his teeth as he recalled the drama that happened just a few months ago with Wolf's girlfriend. He didn't know all the details other than Jazz got herself in trouble with a bunch of online scammers, and they sent someone to kill her. The would-be assassin tried to do that by fire, but Jazz escaped with her nephews, and only her house burned. A total loss. She and Wolf were rebuilding the place as they built a new life together.

There was a showdown of sorts between the assassin, the Slaggers MC, and Wolf, but no one knew what exactly had happened. Wolf was particularly close-mouthed about it. Cam didn't blame him.

A roar of approval pierced the air. Apparently, Ellie decided to go a step further and was shaking her generous rear just inches from the groom's face. He stuck out his tongue as if lapping at the dancer's ass, and his friends egged him on.

Cam nodded toward the stage. "Think we need to do something about that?"

Wolf shook his head. "Not as long as there's no touching. If Ellie gives us the high sign, we'll step in, but she's milking this shit for as many tips as she can get."

Sure enough, Ellie had a G-string full of bills, and not all of them were singles.

Cam grunted. "She's racking up tonight, no doubt."

"I'll keep an eye on them," a voice piped up behind them.

Cam turned to see the newest member of the club. A pair of large, rounded eyes stared up at him from behind thick glasses.

"Yo, Specs."

Specs, as he'd been dubbed, wasn't tall or buff. He was average in appearance and utterly forgettable other than his Coke-bottle glasses, but he had wicked accounting skills and a killer restored Kawasaki Z1 900. His attention to detail and love of spreadsheets got him into the business, and the beautiful bike got him into the club.

Wolf nodded at the short man. "I think it's under control, but stay vigilant. Let me know if Ellie heads over to the hotel, yeah?"

"Roger Dodger!" Specs saluted and darted off toward the bachelor party.

Wolf laughed at the guy, then stiffened up. "Incoming. Check the front door."

Cam glanced over and saw the commotion building. *Shit!* The cute blonde was back and sounded determined as ever to get Scrap's attention.

He hurried over to the door, where Crossman was having trouble containing the woman. He noted that her hair was long and lushly gold with a little wave in it. Very different from the twin braids she wore the first time he saw her. Before he could get there, she'd already pushed her way past Crossman with a determined stride for the table where Scrap usually sat.

Cam blocked her halfway through the room. "He's not here tonight, baby."

If looks could kill, her glare would have incinerated him on the spot. "I'm not 'baby.' My name is Sabrina, and I want to see that old goat ASAP."

She moved to go around him, and he blocked her again. "I get it, *Sabrina*. But again, he's not here."

"Where is he?"

"I have no clue. I don't run his schedule. All's I can tell you is he's not here."

"You've said that three times."

"I'll say it three more if I have to."

Her eyes blazed with icy blue fire, her shoulders set back with defiance. "I'm not leaving this city until I get some answers."

There was an undertone in her voice that Cam recognized. She was putting up a good front, but somewhere in there, she was in pain. It couldn't have been easy, losing one father, finding out you might have another one, and then traveling such a long distance only to be stymied. His instincts told him there was more to this story. He could relate to that and wanted to find out more, but at the moment, he needed to focus on keeping peace in the club.

He held up his hands, palms out. "Listen, I get it. I wish he would take the test and get this settled. But until he gets his head out of his ass, I'm afraid he's gonna dig in."

Her full lips pressed together in irritation. Cam

barely held back his laugh, as her face mirrored the stubborn expression Scrap often wore. It wouldn't be a surprise at all to find out they were blood relatives.

"Look, I'll do what I can, yeah?" he told her.

Her mouth relaxed. "I'm not gonna stop coming here to look for him."

"I don't expect you to."

She didn't speak for a few moments, but she didn't drop her direct stare into his eyes either. Cam's body warmed as he became more aware of her. The firm stance showed off her hourglass figure. Her leather riding jacket covered a simple tunic top that clung to her body, enveloping curves that would make a man weep in gratitude. The V-neck was modest by most standards, with just a hint of cleavage—but enough to make Cam look away so he wouldn't get caught staring. Tight jeans and black boots completed the ensemble. She was a vision from head to toe.

Fuck, Cam thought. *The last thing you need is to be lusting after the ex-prez's daughter.*

Yeah, he might as well admit it. He already believed she *was* Scrap's kid. A DNA test would simply confirm it.

"Yo, we got some new talent up in here!" A drunk-as-hell man stumbled up and shoved Cam out of the way to stand in front of Sabrina. "Whassup, baby? Yous auditioning tonight? I gots some money."

Leering at her, he took a handful of bills and stuffed them down her shirt.

"Motherfuc—" Cam tried to stop him, but he was too late.

"You son of a bitch!" Sabrina let loose on the man with a powerful right hook. The drunk went down.

Hard.

It only took a split second before the place exploded.

"What the fuck?"

"Did a stripper just knock out Linus?"

"Hey, you can't do that!"

Shit!

Cam grabbed Sabrina by the arm and forced her to the door. He hated manhandling a woman, but if he didn't get her away from the crowd, things could escalate into something no one wanted or needed. She seemed to get it and didn't fight him as he hurried her out of the building.

He didn't stop until they got to the closed shoe repair shop a few doors down. He pulled them into the recessed doorway between two display windows to hide from anyone on the street.

"You okay?" His breath fogged in the air as he spoke.

Sabrina didn't answer. She pressed her back against the wide glass and hugged herself.

"What the hell were you thinking, punching a man twice your size? You shoulda let me handle his ass."

She stayed silent and compact.

Cam's ire melted. "Look, seriously, are you okay?"

She raised her head and met his concerned gaze. Whatever shadows she had in her eyes disappeared as shutters dropped over them. "I'm just fine. It ain't the first time I've had to fight off an asshole. Ain't gonna be the last."

Her words bothered him. A lot. But he couldn't process that at the moment. Later, he might ponder it, but for now, he needed to get her somewhere safer than here. "Look, Sabrina, it's a strip club. Guys come here to drink and look at naked women. Yeah, things get out of hand sometimes, but we take care of it. Our ladies get spooked by someone, we make sure they're safe."

Her fire returned, and her chin came up. "I ain't one of your ladies."

"You're Scrap's daughter. That makes you one of us."

He'd said it before he could stop himself, and he couldn't take it back.

Sabrina jolted, and for the first time since he met her, it seemed she had nothing to say. She deflated before his eyes as whatever fight she'd mustered up left her.

Cam swore under his breath. "I'm sorry. I should have waited until Scrap gets tested, but I can't see it any other way." He finally recognized her nonresponse and grew alarmed. "Hey, are you okay?"

She rallied. "Yeah. It's just the first time I've been called someone else's daughter besides Ernie. He was my dad, but possibly not my father." She gave a little shake of her head. "It's really fucked up and confusing as hell."

"I'll bet." He paused, and the silence of the street surrounded them. The shoe repair place had a security light, but it was still too dim for him to make out her features. It didn't matter that he couldn't see her expression, though; he'd had similar experiences, and it wasn't a stretch for him to figure out her headspace. "Listen, Sabrina. We can't fix this tonight, but I'll help you as much as I can, yeah?"

She took a sharp breath through her nose and

blew it slowly out of her mouth. Cam's eyes landed on the shadow of her pursed lips, and for a moment, he wondered what they tasted like.

A burst of noise distracted him, and he peeked around the corner. Sure enough, a limo had pulled up outside the bar, and the bachelor party was loading into the back. They had to carry the groom on their shoulders like pallbearers with a casket.

Cam raised a brow. "Huh. I wonder how the bride will feel tomorrow when he shows up hungover as hell."

"I hope she kicks his ass to the curb."

There was such bitterness in her voice that he jerked his attention back to her. His lower spine locked up at the sudden movement, the muscle twisting viciously, sending a wave of pain down his leg. He couldn't move.

"Son of a bitch!" he gritted out and placed a hand on the window just above her shoulder to keep from falling into her.

"You fuc—what's wrong?" Her angry voice did a complete one-eighty when she realized he was in pain, not trying to cop a feel.

"Back. Cramp." His voice was tight, as he had trouble getting air into his lungs.

"Hang on." She maneuvered herself behind him.

"Put both hands up and lean forward. Don't freak out either."

He felt her hands slip under his shirt and touch the skin just above his hip.

"Damn, that's a bad one. Hold still." She dug her thumb into the area, nearly sending him through the top of the alcove.

"Fuck!" he roared as more pain hit his side and leg, burning up and down his nerves like a flash fire.

"Yeah, I know. Just bear with me a few seconds. Breathe."

He sucked in a huge lungful of air and blew it out. Then did it again. And again.

On the fifth or sixth round, the pain began to release. He inhaled deeper and grew lightheaded as he relaxed, resting his forehead against the cold glass. Each breath coated the surface with a blast of steam. He almost forgot about the woman behind him, until he felt her hands move under his shirt, tracing either side of his spine and stroking over his skin. Her fingers trailed upward over his back to his shoulders, and she lightly pressed and squeezed. The touch held an intimacy he hadn't experienced in a long time, and he froze, not knowing what to say or do next.

What the hell is she doing?

"You're really crunchy back here. I bet you've been hurtin' for a while."

Crunchy?

"Yeah, my back is pretty messed up," he ground out as she spread her hands around his sides.

"I can help you with that."

Fuck! I'm getting a boner. "I got... pills."

Her laugh showed her amusement. He bet she knew what was going on with him. "I'm a massage therapist. Not the pretty spa kind either, although I've done that kind of stuff before. I can work on you once for helping me out tonight. If you want, you can come see me for regular appointments while I'm in town. I'm supposed to check out a gig tomorrow morning at a place called Sunstone Healing."

Massage therapist? He hadn't really thought about that as a possibility. Though visions of him naked while she rubbed his back were not helping his current condition. "I've seen the place. It's not far from here. I'll think about it."

Her hands retreated, and he almost sighed in relief. "Suit yourself, but let me tell you, medical massage is different and targeted. I do a lot of myofascial release, which is just what you need. I've been to school, passed my boards and all that happiness. I'm good at what I do."

He waited a minute more to be safe before turning to face her. No way did he want her to see his jeans bulging at the zipper. "I've never had a massage before, so I can't compare it to anything."

A sassy smile broke across her face. "A massage virgin, eh? Oooh, the things I can do for you!"

Shit, stop it! He put his hands in his pockets to make some room in the front of his pants. "I said I'd think about it."

She raised a brow and reached for her own back pocket. "Hopefully, I'll have a space tomorrow and can start building a schedule, but I'll make time for you whenever you need." She handed him a business card. "This is my old card, but it has my cell number on it. Call me anytime you want me to work on you."

Those words echoed in his head. He stared at the offered rectangle, thinking if he reached out his hand, it would change the course of his life. It felt close to a commitment, not just an hour on a massage table. To what extent, he didn't know yet, but once that card was in his hand, there was no going back.

He lifted his arm and took it without comment. If sparks could flare from the tiny card, he would have been burned.

She turned and smarted off over her shoulder as she walked to her parked bike. "Check with me sometime next week. You give me an hour, and I'll make you a new man."

He watched her rounded rear sway down the street.

What the hell have I gotten myself into?

4

Edna Clauson limped awkwardly through the door to the sidewalk, turned, and locked it behind her. The corner convenience store was chock-full of basic groceries, snacks, ice cream, and other small common items people might need. Rather than go to the bigger shopping centers, many neighborhood people opted to get what they needed here. Clauson's had been around for close to sixty years. Edna and Albert had opened the store together just after they married and had been in business ever since. Albert passed away a few years ago, leaving Edna to run the place herself.

"I'm getting too old for this, Al," she groused as she wrestled her fancy seat walker in front of her bulky figure. "I'm almost eighty-five, you know."

Her habit of talking to her husband had not changed since his death. Every night for decades, they closed up shop at eight o'clock and walked to their small house a few blocks into the residential part of the neighborhood. Tonight, she had a lot on her mind to tell him. "Maybe it's time for me to sell. None of the kids are interested in running the store, and let me tell ya, the neighborhood is going to hell. Why, just last week, another coffee shop got vandalized, just like Bill and Madge's place. Someone set off a bomb, can you believe that?"

She grunted in her effort to keep walking up the hill to the row of narrow houses. Only twenty or so feet from the front of her store and her words came out puffier as her breathing became labored. She stopped to rest for a moment and kept talking. "Anyway, I'm getting slower and slower these days. It's just so hard to keep up. Ruby told me she wants me to move closer over in Chambersburg. Says there's a nice retirement place there I can live where she can keep an eye on me. I'm thinking about it. I can see the grandkids more often too. You should see how tall Coral is now. She's still marching in the band with that trumpet we bought her. I think she wants to—"

A loud boom cracked through the air, drowning

out any words she might have said next. Pain radiated through her knees, and she realized she'd fallen onto the unforgiving concrete sidewalk.

"Oh!" she cried as a fireball erupted and shot outward from the store she'd just left. Heat billowed over her, knocking her flat. The walker fell over, spilling her purse and some of its contents.

"Oh no! Oh! Oh no!" Edna tried to roll over, but her legs wouldn't work right. Her chest tightened, and her breaths shortened even more. "Albert! What's happening?"

Two figures walked up to her, but she could only see black work boots. "Please! Oh, please, can you help me?"

One of them stooped and plucked her purse from the ground. Edna watched helplessly as the figure went through her wallet and stole her cash and credit cards. She whimpered as she struggled for air. "Please. You can take it all. Just please, help me!"

The pain stabbed through her chest like a hot knife and spread from her jaw to her left arm. She couldn't get any air into her lungs.

One of the boots reared back, and Edna thought for a moment that the person meant to kick her. With those heavy steel toes, one strike could kill her.

She closed her eyes and waited for the deadly blow. Instead, the boot shoved her over hard, and she cried out as she scraped the skin from her elbows on the rough pavement.

A man cursed at her, "Fucking dried-up cunt!"

A moment later, she heard them walking away. She cracked open her lids to see both sets of feet heading up the sidewalk, leaving her there.

Thank God, they didn't kill me, Albert was her last thought before she passed out.

5

Cam stood outside Sunstone Healing and debated for the thousandth time about going in. Whatever magic Sabrina worked Friday night made him sleep comfortably for the first time in weeks. No other major events messed up his weekend, and he woke up this morning in a good mood. That lasted all of about an hour, until he got to work.

The first job was turning a set of axles for a Chevy Nova, then building out the camshaft for it. Cam's talent for precision machining had earned him his name, but it also meant he got most of that type of work. Forming the discs, then measuring and grinding the spinning lobes took patience as well as accuracy. If the camshaft wasn't as perfectly timed as possible, the engine wouldn't fire right, and all the work would be wasted.

The job was heavy and tedious, and of course before noon, his back seized up again like it had never been released.

Cam sighed. He'd mentioned to Quillon about the free massage, and his boss made him call to book an appointment. Sabrina had chortled with satisfaction, as if she'd expected his call. She had an opening in the late afternoon, and Quillon made him leave early to get it done.

The spa's facade looked like all the other businesses in this strip mall, but he imagined the inside was probably elegant and had perfumed air floating around. He smelled like cutting fluid.

Nope, I'm not going in there.

He turned to leave, pulling out his phone to call and cancel, when an older African American woman walked toward him.

"The sun don't stop moving, babycakes. Let's go." Her colorful skirt flowed around her short, round body as she moved. "Who are you seeing today?"

Cam had no choice, as the woman herded him into the building. "I'm... uh... Sabrina?"

Her brown eyes lit up. "Oh yes, she's my new girl. Sweet as Southern pie. Don't get her riled, though.

I'm Cicely, and I own the place." The beads hanging from her thin braids rattled as she flipped them behind her back. "She'll do you up right."

Cam's body tightened into one big knot as Sabrina came down a hall into the reception area. "I wasn't sure you were gonna make it. I've got the room ready to go, so come on back. How are you doing today?"

She ushered him down another short hall. Yes, indeed, the place smelled exotic—something spicy that reminded him of one of those bath stores with all the lotions and candles and shit.

"I came straight from work, so I'm not exactly clean," he told her.

"Did you shower this morning?"

"I shower at night. I get pretty dirty at the machine shop, and I don't like sleeping in smoodge."

"Nice word. Smoodge. Are you smoodged up right now?"

"Kinda. Oil and grease from the lathes, n'at."

She waved a hand. "Not a problem. My dad used to—"

She stopped speaking, and her face grew serious. "Will Scrap get his panties in a twist if he finds out you came here to see me?"

Cam shook his head. "That's not my problem.

He's a grown man who can handle his own shit." He changed the subject, as he didn't want to think about why she came to Pittsburgh in the first place. "Remember how I said I've never had a massage before? I don't know what to expect."

A grin burst across her face that Cam could only describe as diabolical. "Oh, darlin', just you wait!"

In five minutes, Cam found himself in a room, stripped down to his boxers and lying under a thin sheet on a flat table with his face in a padded donut, wondering about his life choices. Soft music played in the background, and the air had a clean, fresh smell to it.

Sabrina had stepped out for him to get undressed and settled. She knocked softly before coming back in. "Are you ready?" she asked.

Cam noted an amused tone in her voice and became wary. "Yeah?"

At first, he expected her to just rub his back with some oily stuff. He changed his mind quickly when her elbow dug into his left butt cheek.

"Shit!" The word exploded from him before he could stop it.

"Lower back problems stem from your glutes being too tight. I bet your psoas muscle is also a factor."

"So-Ass?" Cam bit out as tears gathered in his eyes.

"Cuss if you want to. It's pronounced 'so-az,' and it's related to the hip flexors. I know this is tough and hurts. You have some really crunchy spots here, so please tell me if it's too much. I can ease off a bit. And a word to the wise? Relax your sphincter."

Cam's attention flew from the pain in his rear to her words. "What? Did you just tell me to relax my butthole?"

She laughed. "Absolutely, sugar. If you loosen that muscle, it will reduce your overall tension and make this massage easier and more effective. Try it. You'll see."

"I'm doubting your intentions."

She laughed again but kept up the pressure on his butt cheek. "I'm a professional. I promise, nothing I do is meant to hurt you, and there are no ulterior motives. You can trust me."

Cam took a breath. "Okay. I'll... um... do my best."

Jeez, how many times had he talked about his butthole with a woman? Up until now, zero.

The pressure she applied was steady, and the muscle gradually released. "I like your ink."

Cam's back tensed at her compliment. He

hadn't thought about what she might find on his back. Most people didn't notice beneath the elaborate tattoo. He hoped she wouldn't either. "Thanks."

The tattoo was a black-and-gray clockface with interlocking gears on the inside and hands that were permanently pointed at four forty. A set of forging hammers crossed over either side of the clock and appeared to be breaking it open. The scripted phrase across his shoulders read "Forget the past. Start over. Every day."

"That's a very specific time. Why did you choose it?"

He hesitated before saying, "It's when I was born." He hoped she picked up on his reluctance to talk. The short answer seemed to work.

She moved from spot to spot, finding trigger points and working them. Cam did his best to keep from tensing up and fighting her. It was hard.

Speaking of hard....

"Tell me about Ernie." He had to keep her talking, more to keep himself distracted than her.

Her breath intake was sharp but didn't sound angry.

"That's kind of a long story. You sure you want to hear it?"

"Yeah." He was genuinely curious about the pretty woman.

She moved to the other side of the table and worked his right butt cheek the same way. His concentration moved from his burgeoning dick to the pain, though he could admit that the left one was a lot looser now.

"I barely remember when my mom and dad were together. She was there, and then she wasn't. For most of my childhood, she would show up whenever she felt like it, stay for a few days, sometimes a few weeks, then disappear again. Ernie didn't divorce her until after I turned eighteen, I guess to see if she'd eventually settle down and be an actual mom to me. But I always wondered how he could stay married to someone who didn't stick around for any length of time."

She shifted to his lower back and spine, pressing her fingers into the tendons just above his butt crack. He bit back a curse and tensed for a moment but forced himself to let it go as he listened to her story.

"I grew up with Ernie and my stepbrother, Rodrigo, Ernie's first wife's son. Ernie adopted him, so legally he's my older brother, but he's never really considered me to be his sister, even though we grew up together after his mom passed away."

She moved around his lower back, working the rigid tight spots and bringing tears to his eyes. "I'd say growing up, it was all pretty normal stuff. We had school and chores. We stayed with Aunt Marianne or Aunt Rosa when Dad had to make a run. In the summers, we traveled with him in the truck sometimes, no summer camps or anything like that. We weren't poor, but there was no extra money for that kind of thing."

Cam could relate. He had also grown up in a household with a tight budget.

"Anyway, if we were broke, no one told me. When we rode with him when we were little, we'd sleep in the cab. Later, Rodrigo decided he didn't want to go anymore and stayed with Aunt Rosa when Ernie had to make a run. Those were some really good times, just me and my dad. The first vehicle I ever drove was an eighteen-wheeler. I wasn't supposed to be behind the wheel, but Dad taught me well. I even thought about following in his footsteps, but I found this profession instead. Dad loved it when I decided to become a massage therapist and helped me all through my school training."

She moved her thumbs down and to the side. It hurt, but in a good way. The oil she used had a pleasant scent that wasn't overpowering or flowery. She repeated the motion several times, loosening the tightness and bringing relief. Cam found himself drifting into a dream state despite the pressure she applied. He felt good.

Almost too good.

She started feeling up his spine and found a bad spot just under his shoulder blade. He winced as she applied pressure and movement. Talking was a great distraction, and he did his best to keep up the conversation. His curiosity about the woman had nothing to do with his need to hear her voice. "Sounds like you and your dad had a good life. How come you wanted to find Scrap?"

"I debated a long time about that. I'm really not sure, to tell you the truth. The man has done nothing for me my whole life, never acknowledged my existence. That's either because he didn't believe Raquel or maybe he didn't know about me in the first place. I think I just have this need to find out for sure."

Her hands moved to the other side of his shoulder and started on another spot. "I spent most of my life feeling odd, like I didn't really belong. I wasn't abused or starved or anything, but I wasn't exactly welcome at times. Aunt Rosa would call me 'that woman's daughter' instead of her niece. After Ernie died and it came out that Walter might be my real father, she turned against me and called me a bunch of other names. 'Bastard' and 'leech' were two of them. She said if I wasn't really blood related, I had no place there and should get out. So now I guess I'm looking for where I'm supposed to be."

"What happened to your Aunt Marianne?"

Sabrina smoothed more oil onto her hands. "She passed away a few years ago. They said it was a stroke. My cousins had a time getting the estate settled. Ernie talked to me about writing a will, but he never did. He died a few months ago without ever taking care of it, and the family has been in an uproar ever since. Lots of drama and finger-pointing, mainly at me, saying if I'm not his bio-daughter, then I have no claim to anything. Personally, I don't care about any of it. I'd give away anything my dad left me just to have him back."

Cam felt her hands shaking as they applied pressure to the tendons just under his armpits. It hurt like hell, but the release was incredible. "I'm sorry that happened to you. I'll try to help you get Scrap to come around so at least you'll have that answer. He's a stubborn old goat, though, so be ready for a fight."

Her light laugh was good to hear. "Thanks. I

appreciate your efforts." She lifted her hands and took a step back. "Okay, time to flip. Scooch down until your head is on the table."

Cam noticed that she looked to the corner of the room as she lifted the sheet from his hips. He turned over, and she settled the sheet over his body once more.

"Now, this one may get a little intense, so please don't be afraid to tell me if it's too much." She dug her fingers into the pocket between his hip, groin, and thigh.

"Fuck!" he cried out.

"Yeah, this is a bad one. I'll ease off a bit. Take some deep breaths and try to relax."

Cam sucked in several lungfuls of air, enough to make him dizzy. The sharp burning in his thigh distracted him enough that it took him several minutes to figure out how close her hands were to his dick. This time, any twitch of interest disappeared as his focus squared entirely on the stressed muscle. He needed more distraction. "Do you think you'll go back to Florida after you find out what you need to know?"

She paused. "I'm not sure yet. I could go home—or what home I have left. I could stay here. I could leave and explore the country until I find a place I like. I have a lot of paths in front of me. I don't understand yet where they'll lead, but I can't move on until I figure out who I am."

Cam agreed with her. "I get it. Like I said, I'll help you as much as I can."

She moved to his other side and repeated the dig. "That's great, Camshaft. Hey, do you have another name besides your road name?"

"Yeah, but I don't use it or answer to it. You can just call me Cam." The pain was just as intense, but he didn't yell this time as he'd expected it.

"Wanna share it anyway?"

"No." His tone was brusque.

"Okay, then. You're done. I'll step out while you get dressed."

A few minutes later, Cam walked down the short hall to where Sabrina waited.

"How do you feel?" she asked, her head cocked to the side.

He rolled his shoulders. For the first time in days, he was pain-free. "I'm a little sore, but I'm good." He grinned. "You weren't kidding."

Her sassy smile came out at that. *Damn, she's cute!*

"I never kid when it comes to massage. Today was a freebie, but next time, I'm gonna charge full price for working on your ass. I expect a good tip too."

Cam let out a bark of laughter. "How do you know I'll be back?"

Her mouth curved even more. "Oh, sugar, you'll definitely be back."

6

The seven senior members of the Iron City Knights MC sat or stood at the rounded table near the back of the club. The patch-overs from earlier this year had taken off back to where they came from, since the club was going through some serious restructuring. Baghouse, Melter, and Quillon perched on stools, while Camshaft and Crossman stood nearby. Scrap still sat on his throne, sullen and silent, but the new president, Wolf, was running the show now. He slammed his hand on the scarred wood surface in lieu of a gavel. "Let's come to order and get this shit done."

Cam held back a smirk at their version of Robert's Rules. Today was not a day for amusement, as there were serious issues that needed to be addressed.

"Between the machine shop and forge next door, which stay open during the day, and Attic, which is open at night, we have people at our places almost all the time. There are very few hours when no one is around." Wolf paused and sipped from a silver Yeti go-cup. "We're pretty much covered, but there's still shit going on in the area we need to know about. Take a look at the security camera footage from Justin and Rorrie's coffee shop a couple streets over." He clicked the remote in his hand, and the flat-screen TV on the wall came to life.

The images were blurred and grainy but clear enough to show two figures walking up to the window of the business and then shattering it with swinging bats. One spray-painted a big red X on the front door before tossing something through the broken glass. A moment later, the video showed them running away as a bright flash exploded across the screen.

"As luck would have it, the sprinkler system came on and doused the fire before it spread to another building. There's still a lot of damage, though." He turned the TV off and dropped the remote onto the table. "Who or what does this remind you of?"

Cam's mouth turned down. Not too many months ago, the vape and head shop across the street from the club was bombed out in the same way. Unfortunately, the owner, who they called "the hippie guy," was there, and the blast had killed him. A shudder ran through Cam as he remembered the sight and smell of the man's burnt, twisted body.

Scrap also squirmed in his chair. The older man never had much to say when he previously ran church meetings, but today he was noticeably silent. His chin almost rested on his chest, and he seemed to either be asleep or drifting toward it.

"Clauson's store got bombed the same way a couple days ago. Edna's banged up but okay." Wolf leaned back. "Our buddy Officer Denny took charge and told me there's no camera or CCTV footage. I bet Jazz can find something, though. It sounds like the same pattern."

"It can't be the Slaggers again. Your girl did a number on them, and they disbanded," Melter piped up as he sprinkled some ground-up leaves onto a white paper.

Cam found himself in agreement with the older man. Jazz had mad hacker skills and used them to screw up the Slaggers' finances, which crippled the rival MC. Despite their retaliation, they never got their money back, and the Knights assumed they were gone for good.

Wolf's eyebrows came together. "Are you seriously rolling a joint right now?"

Melter glanced up in surprise. "Yeah. What's the problem?"

"We're having a meeting."

"So what?"

Wolf lost his temper. "Whattaya mean, 'So what?' We're trying to revamp and restructure this club. You wanna get high, do it on your own time!"

"It's just weed, man."

"I don't care if it's fucking gold. Do that shit later."

Melter mumbled something under his breath, but he relented and tucked the joint into the front pocket of his shirt.

Wolf resumed the meeting. "We don't know who's behind this, and after the shit show we just dealt with, I'm not taking chances. The businesses and people who live here are looking to us to be leaders and help protect them. We're not going all vigilante, but we will start supporting our turf more."

Baghouse scoffed. "Yinz think we're a neighborhood watch or some shit like that?"

Wolf's face turned to steel. "Yeah, that's the plan. You got a problem with it?"

The older man scoffed. "Fuck no. If some jagoffs want to get in our faces, we need to start pushin' back."

Wolf's expression relaxed at that; having a founding member like Baghouse on board made this task easier. "I'm not talking about patrolling the streets on a regular basis. We don't have the manpower for that. I'm saying we keep our eyes open and be present, like getting coffee at Justin and Rorrie's place when they open back up. People see us somewhere, they're less likely to target the place. If one of our people gets wind of something, that's when we act."

"What if our presence puts a target on someone's back?" Crossman asked.

Cam's eyebrow rose as he agreed. "He's got a point. Suppose the goal is to fuck with us by messing with the people around us. Ever since Bill and Madge had to close down Coffee and Cakes, we've been going to Justin and Rorrie's to get caffeinated. Hell, all of us visit Clauson's for stuff. What if that's the reason they got hit?"

Wolf paused and tapped his fingers on the tabletop. "It's a possibility. Then again, it's also possible they got hit for something else. All's I'm saying is we need to be alert and pay attention to the people in our area. If we hear about something or someone gets a threat, we need to step in and step up. Make sense?"

A chorus of "Yeahs" sounded around the table, along with some nods.

"Anyone else got any new business?" Wolf paused and glanced around the room. "Right. Adjourned." He slapped his palm on the table and rose, then groaned and grabbed the small of his back. "Shit!"

Cam noticed and cringed. "You oughta lay off working on the new house so much. Just let the crew get it done."

Wolf straightened and blew out a breath. "It's not that. It's swinging Jazz's nephews around at the park yesterday. Those little shits are heavier than they think."

"Stuck with babysitting, eh? They're not that big."

Wolf grunted. "Huh. You try to swing a five-year-old and a three-year-old around for a couple hours. I guarantee your back will feel it too."

Cam laughed. "Sabrina can take care of that for you. She's really good."

"Who the hell is Sabrina?" Melter asked as he pulled out the joint he'd rolled earlier. He put one end in his mouth and started to light it.

"Scrap's daughter." Wolf frowned. "Take that shit outside."

Scrap came awake at Wolf's words, and his mouth twisted in irritation.

Shit, Cam mentally cursed. It wasn't his business what the deal was between Sabrina and Scrap, but he thought she had the right to know if he was her real father.

Melter's eyes glowed with anger and confusion. He shrugged, lifting his hands in the air. "What the fuck? No one's had a problem with it before."

"Well, there's a problem now. This is a legit business, and we need to keep it that way. I don't care if you want to get stoned, but you don't do that here. Got it?"

"Gawddammit, I don't have a fuckin' daughter!" Scrap bellowed, punctuated by a fist to the surface of the table. The pieces on the ever-present chess board fell over.

Cam wanted to yell back at the stubborn man, but he kept his tone low and, he hoped, reasonable.

"It only takes a minute to find out for sure. Just take the damn DNA test and be done with it."

"I ain't takin' no fuckin' test! Whoever the fuck she is, she ain't mine!"

At one time, the garbled growl from the most senior member of the club would have shut everyone up. Not so much anymore.

Cam rolled his eyes. "Whatever you say, Scrap. I hope you don't regret those words, 'cause this thing is gonna eat at you until you give in and do that cheek swab."

Wolf scratched his bearded chin with two fingers. "I don't get why you're being so damn pigheaded about it, unless you think there might be a chance she *is* your daughter."

Scrap's face turned beet red in anger, and he spluttered a few times before he found his words. "Yinz can piss up a fuckin' rope, ya gawddamn jagoffs! I've said already I don't have a fuckin' daughter!"

As Scrap's roar reverberated through the building, the other members of the Iron City Knights watched silently as the old man fell to the floor in a boneless heap.

7

Sabrina pulled the bottom sheet from the massage table with an exaggerated swoosh. Only a few days into joining this group, and she had a growing roster of clients coming to see her. As her reputation for medical massage rose, her bank account would too. Her living expenses were minimal, and she could bank the majority of her pay and tips. The commute wasn't bad either, as Cicely allowed her to park her rig in the scrappy lot behind the storefront. All she had to do was unlock the back door of the spa to get to the bathroom and mudroom, which was equipped with a shower—all the amenities she really needed for now. The weather was getting colder, and even though she could still ride her bike, soon she would have to park it in the trailer and take the public transit system to wherever she needed to go besides work.

She clicked on the table warmer and stepped out to the front to wait for her next client. He was a new one, another older steel worker complaining of back, shoulder, and arm pain. Not uncommon for someone who makes a living working with their hands and body.

"Have fun with this one," Stephan remarked with a snarky smile. "He's real special."

Stephan's clients came to see him for relaxing Swedish massages, body wraps, facials, and gossip. People who needed targeted deep tissue came to Sabrina's table. Not the same style or clientele, and yet the tiny man resented her presence all the same. Still, it didn't help her to aggravate a senior employee. She could get her digs back in other ways.

"Thanks for the tip, Steph," she said with an overly sweet smile. She knew the man hated having his name shortened and preferred to be called Stephan. Oh well!

His upper lip curled, and he gave her "the look" before turning to sashay away. All he needed was a finger snap to complete the act. Sabrina suppressed her amusement but stuck out her tongue at his receding back.

Her phone dinged with a new text. She slipped the device from her back pocket, intent on muting it for the upcoming session, but the sender caught her eye. Dread bloomed in her stomach, and her heartbeat increased. She debated ignoring the message until after work, but experience had taught her that he would just keep texting over and over again until she responded. Her client hadn't arrived yet, so she had some time.

Sabrina inhaled as deeply as she could through her nose and slowly blew out through pursed lips. She repeated the act twice, opening her diaphragm and keeping each cycle even. The relaxed breathing exercise helped, and she tapped open the message.

> Rodrigo: I need you to sign some papers.

Her chest tightened back up, and she tried the exercise again. Didn't help this time.

> Sabrina: Why?

> Rodrigo: Aunt Rosa is making noises about the inheritance shit.

She huffed at the words on the screen. Funerals could bring out the worst in families, and apparently, hers was no exception. The day of Ernie's funeral, she and her brother had gotten into a huge fight. He ended up with the family behind him, and she was out on her own.

> Sabrina: What does that have to do with me? You said to get the fuck out and not come back.

> Rodrigo: I made a mistake.

Made a mistake, eh? Must have been a big one for you to break down and contact me.

Her stomach churned with several emotions. Mostly anxiety with a bit of righteousness, as she'd stated many times before she left Florida that there was more to be done for their father's estate, but no one wanted to listen.

> Sabrina: Send them to me via Google Docs and I'll read them when I get a chance.

> Rodrigo: I'm not sending shit over the internet. You gotta come here to do it.

Anger replaced her anxiety as her thumbs flew over the screen.

> Sabrina: I don't have to do squat for you. You need papers signed, you can bring them to me.

> Rodrigo: You always were a fucking cunt.

> Sabrina: And you were always a fucking asshole. I guess things haven't changed much.

She closed the messaging app before she could read another text from him and powered down the phone. Her hands shook from excess adrenaline, as they always did when dealing with her stepbrother. The decades-long rivalry had ramped up to epic proportions after their father's death. Apparently, that was still going on.

"Hey, Sabrina! Your client is here," Stephan called back.

She took several more deep, healing breaths to regulate herself and get her focus back. It was damn near impossible, but she had a workday to get through.

The man lumbered in, tall and burly. He was slightly larger than a dad bod, but that didn't matter, as he was clearly as strong as an ox. And he had a healthy ego to match if the smirk on his face was any indication. "Hello, little lady. I'm Frank. You think you can take me on?"

Sabrina ignored the innuendo. This wasn't her first rodeo with ambitious men. "No prob. What are we working on today? Back and shoulders, right?"

"I'll let you work on anything you want."

Obvious much? She faked a big smile while cussing him under her breath. "You listed your back on the intake form, so let's start there. I'll step out for a minute while you get changed. Face down on the table. I'll be right back."

Sabrina exited, closed the door, and leaned back against the wall outside the room. Some female massage therapists only wanted to work on women. She understood why, as it was exhausting to deal with these types of men, but she was new in the area and needed to take whoever came to her room.

It's temporary, girl. If you can handle those redneck dock workers in Sarasota, you can handle this guy.

But how temporary would it be? She was here to find answers, but so far, Scrap refused to do anything. She had no family or friends, but then again, she had no one back in Florida either, except for Amelia. Her limbo state had been annoying at first, but it was taking a real toll now. It was hard to keep a positive outlook when everything around her had turned to shit.

Cam came to her mind, along with the tattoo on his back. The crossed hammers and the broken clock were simple, but the time it showed still held her curiosity. His chosen phrase also had some meaning to him: "Forget the past. Start over. Every day."

It must have something to do with the scars she'd felt under her fingers that day.

Sabrina believed he'd been through some serious shit in his life to put that saying on his body. She could definitely relate, and a part of her wanted to hear his story. Perhaps he would share it with her one day. So far, their encounters had been friendly and even a bit flirtatious on her side. He was a good-looking man, and when he was on her table, she'd noticed his body's reaction to her touch. The boner he sported was impressive, but he didn't try to mess with her over it. He did the gentlemanly thing and ignored it until it subsided. Even though he wore an Iron City Knights cut, he was in her corner.

Her instincts told her Frank wasn't going to be that noble.

She shook her head to get back to the task at hand. She rapped her knuckles against the door and entered when Frank called out. It didn't take her very long to see the man was totally naked under the blanket. Sabrina gritted her teeth, but she did most of her work covered, so if this guy wanted to go commando, no harm. Yet.

"You can dig in as much as you want to. I'm a tough guy. You can't hurt me," Frank teased.

Wanna bet?

"Well, the goal isn't to hurt you but to release any tension you have." She used her most neutral voice, even though she could already see where this was going. As long as the dude stuck to a flirty vibe only and kept his hands to himself, she could handle him.

Of course, that was too much to ask.

She started mapping as she usually did, and as she moved around the table, she felt the brush of his hand against her hip. Her jaw tightened as she tamped down on her urge to smack him. Sometimes, people made touches by mistake. This one she let go for the moment, just in case. Men could talk a good game, but they typically failed at the follow-through.

Unfortunately, the would-be Romeo took her silence for acquiescence. This time, he flat-out stroked and then cupped her hip in his bowl-like hand.

Sabrina leaned over and planted an elbow in the

spot near his spine, quickly hiding the smile that spread on her face when he yelped. "Too much pressure? Must be a bad trigger point."

"Nope," Frank ground out. "It's fine. I can take it."

Yeah, I bet you can.

"This is a really crunchy area. Let me know if it's too much, okay?"

Sabrina felt his body flinch beneath her, but he did remove his hand from her hip.

An hour later, Frank was sweating and breathing hard, but all the knots in his shoulder and back were gone. He had tried twice more to put his hands on her as she worked, and both times, she'd found a trigger point that made him rethink those decisions.

"You're a lot stronger than you look," he remarked warily as she was about to leave the room so he could get dressed.

Sabrina put on her sticky-sugar Southern-belle smile and simpered at him. "Aw, it's so sweet of you to say that!"

She paused to turn her phone back on before cleaning the room and changing the sheets on the table. A dozen notification bells rang one after another. She smirked as she guessed that most, if not all, of those texts came from her brother cursing her to hell and back. She might check them later or simply delete them altogether. He could either speak to her with a civil tongue or not at all.

Cicely came in as she was finishing up. Her mouth was in a deep frown, her sculpted brows narrowed. "That guy who just left—what did you do to him?"

Sabrina blinked. "Just a routine mapping and massage. Why?"

"He said you touched him inappropriately and he's gonna leave a bad Yelp review."

Anger flared up in her chest. "I did what? Absolutely not! That nutjob tried to feel *me* up!"

Cicely took a deep breath. "Are you sure he didn't just, um, brush against you or something?"

Sabrina was shocked. Never had a supervisor or someone she worked with questioned her integrity like this. "I don't know how you do things up here, but in Sarasota, when a man cups a woman's hip, it's usually considered deliberate."

Cicely raised her chin and blew out a breath toward the ceiling, as if asking for guidance. "Okay, I won't assign him to you again. But if I get another bad customer review naming you, I'll have to let you go. Understand?"

Sabrina bit her lip and nodded. "Yes, ma'am, I get it."

She finished cleaning and prepping the room for the next client, but her mind was elsewhere. Was this a sign that she needed to move on?

Rodrigo's texts came back to her. There was nothing back in Florida for her either. Perhaps it was time she gave up on Scrap and his refusal to take the test, loaded up her van, and left. It wasn't like she'd put roots down in this city that obviously didn't want her. The only person so far who seemed to have any welcome for her at all was Cam, and even that was still limited.

No family, no friends, and a workplace that was slowly turning toxic. Perhaps it *was* time to throw in the towel and move on. Surely there was a place for her somewhere.

A blast of heavy metal music came from her back pocket, and she pulled out her phone. Cam's number flashed across the screen. With a sense of dread, she answered. "Hey, stranger. Weird that I was just thinking about you."

"I hope you're not with a client. I didn't want to text this news, so I took a chance and called. Scrap collapsed during a meeting and is on his way to the hospital. Thought you should know."

Sabrina's heart stuttered as emotions warred inside her chest. She swung like a pendulum between *serves the bastard right* to *please don't die!* "Where—" She stopped and swallowed the lump lodged in her throat. "Where is he?"

"West Penn."

Tears filled her eyes, and she pressed a fist to her mouth to keep it still. Thoughts full of anger, worry, justification, confusion, and fear circled in her mind like a merry-go-round, and she wanted to scream, cry, or both at the same time. She swallowed the ball of emotions, leaving them sitting in her gut like a lump of iron ore. "Should… should I go there?"

"It's up to you. No judgment from me."

"I, um… I think I will. What's the address?"

Cam's voice calmed some of the chaos in her brain. "You're at work, right? Got your helmet?"

"Yes."

"You're not far from the club. I'll come get you, yeah?"

"You don't have to—"

He interrupted her with a gentle but firm tone. "I don't have to do a damn thing, but I'm going to. Stay put. I'll be right there."

8

THE SPRAWLING HOSPITAL TOOK UP MORE THAN A CITY block with its multiple buildings and parking structures. Cam drove past the deck and parked at the convenience store across the street. Sabrina rode comfortably behind him. His awareness of her arms around him lingered even after she dismounted from the bike, but at the moment, they had bigger things to worry about. He said a few words to the day manager to keep an eye on his bike. A hundred-dollar bill helped. He still didn't like leaving it there, but it was safer than the parking deck. Anyone who recognized his bike might want to mess with it. Until the club figured out what was happening in their area, vigilance remained a priority.

The ER's waiting room was full of people, but

they gave a wide berth to the two bikers who stood in full regalia near the entrance. Cam approached with Sabrina's hand tucked firmly in his. "What'd they say?"

Quillon gave a big sigh. "Not a lot. EKG is normal, so they don't think it's his heart, but his blood pressure is through the roof. They're running more tests."

Baghouse grunted and picked at a dry cuticle. "Last time he was in a hospital, he'd just had the accident. Hell, not even the kidney stones made him come here."

Quillon blinked. "When did he have kidney stones?"

"He's had 'em a couple times. Once last year. Pretty fuckin' bad," Baghouse answered gruffly.

The door to the cubicles opened, and colorful curses floated through.

"Gawddammit! Don't you fuckin' stick another needle in me!"

A corner of Quillon's mouth twitched. "Yeah, he's not exactly cooperating. A heart attack sounds right to me."

Sabrina grunted. "You have to have a heart before you can have a heart attack. I bet his is missing."

Cam heard her words, but her rigid posture belied the notion that she didn't care. One glance at her fidgeting hands confirmed she felt this deeply. Perhaps she was worried she wouldn't get her answers if Scrap suddenly died, but Cam didn't buy that idea. Sabrina didn't strike him as a selfish mercenary. She might be mad as hell at the old man, but she didn't wish him ill.

"Convenient as it is, I don't think now is the time to ask about that cheek swab. He's likely to bite your head off, chew it, and swallow before you got the words out," Quillon stated.

"I wasn't planning on it, sugar," Sabrina returned. "I'm not gonna kick a man while he's down, even if he *is* an asshole. I do want to know, though. As soon as possible."

"I get that. When he's stable and in a better mood, I'll talk to him and see if he'll take the test. Right now, he's snapping and growling like a street dog, but I'm betting this episode or whatever it is scared him too."

The doors opened and a young man in scrubs came through, peeling off his mask as he approached. "Family for Walter... uh... Scrap?"

Quillon lifted a finger. Sabrina stayed silent, but her grip on Cam's hand tightened.

"We need to keep your friend overnight. There's minor fluid buildup around his heart and lungs, and we'd like to get that inflammation under control before we send him home."

Cam's mouth tightened into a grim line as he listened to the doctor, who looked all of twelve years old. "So, what does that mean? Did he have a heart attack after all?"

The kid shook his head. "No, the EKG and enzymes show no cardiac arrest, but the extra fluid is concerning. There are some possible serious conditions like congestive heart failure or a diabetes complication, or it could be from injury or a benign tumor. We don't know yet. He'll stay here for observation, and we'll keep you as informed as we can. The patient does not want to share his personal information, and under HIPAA, we have to honor his privacy."

A nurse came up and grabbed the doctor's attention as he turned away from the group of bikers.

Quillon pulled out his phone and started tapping on the screen. "I'm texting Wolf. He's on duty at the bar tonight. Crossman and Ratchet are there too. It's been pretty slow, so we're covered if you want to take the night off, Cam. Stalemate is on standby."

Cam grunted and scratched the back of his neck. The muscles in his shoulder had already tightened back up, and he made a mental note to book an appointment with Sabrina ASAP. "You're right. I think we'll get goin' and check back in tomorrow."

Quillon nodded. "Sounds like a plan. I'll be in touch."

Sabrina was quiet as she followed Cam back to where he'd parked the bike. It looked just like he left it, and some of his anxiety faded. He flicked two fingers at the clerk and pulled the lizard helmet from the locked saddlebag. Sabrina took it and put it on her head.

"Where are we going?" he asked as he strapped his own helmet on.

"Back to the spa."

Cam mounted and held the bike steady for her to climb on behind him. He settled into the cradle of her thighs and fired up the engine. She leaned forward and placed her arms around his waist, holding on lightly as they took off through the city streets and headed toward her workplace.

The ride wasn't that exciting. Buildings and businesses lined the route, and pedestrians on the sidewalks paid little attention to them. The traffic lights kept them from going very fast, and they had to stop for a string of red lights. At each one, he'd stop the motorcycle and steady it with one leg while Sabrina clung to him. He could tell this wasn't the first time she'd been on the back of a bike.

But it was the first time with him. The last woman to be on the bike with him? A long-ass time ago, and a memory he'd just as soon not bring back.

He wondered how long it would be before Sabrina's patience gave out about the DNA test, but he admired her for not pushing it right now. Cam had no idea how serious this situation was, but Scrap wasn't a young man anymore. He bet that was the biggest reason the doctor wanted to keep him there overnight.

Pulling up to the massage business, Cam waited for Sabrina to dismount before he swung one long leg over and off the bike. He lifted his helmet's face shield as he regarded the dark storefront. "Looks closed. Do you have appointments this late?"

"No, I'm camping in the back." She took off her helmet, shook out her long mane, and ran her fingers through the tangles.

He shook his head. "Come again?"

She tucked her headgear under her arm. "My van is in the back lot."

"Your van?"

Her face showed annoyance. "Yeah, sugar, my van."

They stared at each other for a moment. This business and the others like it on this strip had some employee parking behind the buildings, but the only way to get to it was a one-way alley at the end of the block. Unless she went through the building, Sabrina had to walk all the way to the end of the street to get to her "van."

Cam was dying to see what she had set up. He pulled off his helmet but left the bandana he'd tied around his forehead. "Mind if I take a look?"

She huffed and rolled her eyes. "I don't see why you need to, but okay."

Sabrina turned and typed in the combination for the front door, and the electronic lock granted them access. The place was dark, but she led the way through, using her phone as a flashlight. The back of the building was more spacious than he thought, and sure enough, there was a van with a small trailer parked close to the outer side wall.

Dread bloomed in his stomach. "Is this what I think it is?"

"What do you mean?"

"Are you living in your car?"

"It's a van, and yes, I live in it. What's the problem?"

"It isn't safe."

Her stance snapped into a stone-cold stillness. "I've camped at Walmarts, gyms, and truck stops and never had any problems. This place is well hidden. I'm just as safe here as I am anywhere else."

"It's isolated. No one else is around to help you if you have trouble."

Her mouth broke into a smile he was sure she meant to be sarcastic. "You worried about me, sugar?"

"Yes."

The one-word answer seemed to catch her off guard. "Well, I thank you for your concern, but I'm a grown-ass woman who can take care of herself."

Cam's eyes went back to her rig. He had extra rooms at his place, and it was on the tip of his tongue to offer that to her, but how would she take it? Like he was making a move on her? Yeah, he was attracted to her, but too much shit was happening right now for him to think about that.

He thought of a compromise instead. "Park at the club. Someone is there almost all the time. I work a lot of nights there, so if you need me, I'll be close by."

Sabrina's smile didn't meet her eyes. "I'll think about it."

He heard her dismissal loud and clear. Yes, she was a perfectly capable woman, but he still hated the idea of her being out here by herself. If something happened to Sabrina...

Someone would die.

He was startled by the sudden surge of anger at just thinking about a threat to this woman. The level of possessiveness wasn't familiar, and he didn't know how to react.

"It would mean a lot to me if you'd park at the club."

"I said I'd think about it."

He tried again. "It's not just about you, babe. I'll go nuts if I can't know you're safe."

She cocked her head to one side. "So, this is more for your mental health?"

"Yeah." He was willing to say anything to get her out of there.

He held his breath, wondering if stubbornness really was a hereditary trait.

She sighed. "Well, sugar, it's real convenient to be where I am, but I'll check out some spots around y'all's bar and let you know."

Cam figured this was the most concession he

would get from her. "You've got my number. Promise me you'll use it if you need anything, yeah?"

He expected her to bristle, but she surprised him with a nod. "I will. Promise."

She unlocked the side door of her van before turning back to him. "If you hear anything about Scrap tonight, would you mind texting me?"

"Yeah, I can do that."

She hesitated in opening the door. She didn't seem to be scared of him; it was more anticipatory, like she didn't understand what came next. Cam remembered this as being the moment during a high school date when you tried to determine whether or not a good night kiss was in order. More than once he'd stood on a girl's front porch and wondered if he should lean in and take one. If this had been a date, maybe he would take the chance, but too much had happened today, and it wasn't the right time.

Yet.

"Good night, Sabrina."

"'Night, Cam."

It was all he could do to mount up and drive away after hearing his name on her tongue.

9

The glowing billet of steel threw off sparks as Cam pressed it in the hydraulic machine. The power hammer was still broken and the work was slow, but the manual press helped. He'd cut and layered twenty-five pieces of sheet steel and copper, then forge welded them into one block. He repeated this process as he heated, flattened, and folded the piece until he had two hundred layers. The technique was called Damascus, and when he finished this set of knives, they would be gorgeous with their distinctive forging pattern.

It took a lot of time, but in the end, he would have something really special.

Quillon brushed steel shavings from one of the

lathes. "Nice-looking piece. I can't wait to see the colors when you're done with it. Competition knife?"

Cam lifted his foot and pushed down on the operation pedal. The press lowered, forcing the orange metal to combine. "Don't know. I might enter something in one of those blade competitions someday. Right now, I'm just experimenting."

He paused after a few minutes and swiped a hand over his forehead. The heat of the forge and the exertion of using the large machining tool made him sweat. "Will someone fix the power hammer soon?"

"The new part is still backordered. I called yesterday, and the guy said two weeks."

"That's what he said two weeks ago."

Quillon finished cleaning one lathe, then moved to another one. "I told him that too. Also told him if that part stays backordered much longer, we'll be doing business with someone else."

Cam pulled the pressed billet from the machine and examined the results. He then put it back in the furnace to reheat for another fold. "I do appreciate a great hand-hammered finish, but I wouldn't mind a break from the anvil."

"I hear you."

The men worked in silence for a few minutes

with only the low thunder of the furnace between them. Cam completed two more folds before taking a break. Quillon waited until Cam laid the final billet on the anvil before speaking again.

"The hospital sent Scrap home this morning. He's still refusing to take the DNA test."

Cam shook his head and grabbed a cold bottle of water from the fridge. "I don't see the big deal. Five minutes out of his life isn't that much to ask."

"I think it's more than that."

Cam paused. "What do you mean?"

Quillon dumped the last of the shavings into a bin that was already full of scraps. Metal never went to waste here; it was either used in making billets for blades or for other forging projects, or it went to the recycling plant. "Put yourself in Scrap's shoes. How would you react if you found out about a daughter you didn't know about for twenty-some years?"

That gave Cam pause. He hadn't thought about it from Scrap's point of view. "You saying Scrap feels guilty or something?"

Quillon broke down the tooling on the lathe, removing the cutting bits, cleaning, and storing them. "Something like that. I keep wondering how I'd feel about it if I found out my kid was raised by another man. Did she have enough? Was she taken care of like she deserved?" He popped the lid onto the bin. "It would kill me to think I wasn't there for her."

"So why deny her?"

The older biker shrugged. "Probably easier that way than to admit he abandoned his child."

Cam shook his head. "I'm not sure that's valid. Maybe Raquel never even told him about Sabrina. If she didn't, how was he supposed to know?"

"Toss me a water, yeah?"

Cam lobbed a bottle at Quillon, who caught it and snapped off the lid. "I don't have any answers. I just figure he's dealing with this shit as best he can. It's affecting him, too, almost as bad as it is Sabrina."

"So, what are we supposed to do about it?"

"Nothing."

Cam dropped his empty bottle into the plastic recycle bin. "Are you serious? Nothing?"

Quillon's phone beeped. He took it out and grinned broadly before texting back. His amused smile told Cam it was probably his wife, Tracie. "Yeah. I'm looking at it from my perspective. If some kid showed up at my doorstep out of the blue, claiming I was their daddy, I'd be pissed, but I'd want answers. I expect Scrap will get there."

"I hope so. Sabrina needs them."

"You like her, don't you?"

Cam paused from putting tools away and cooling down the furnace. His mind cued up a movie of the times he'd been around her. He pictured the curvaceous blonde on the red bike with that ridiculous helmet on her head. Then came the night he pulled her from a potential club fight. Later, her cuteness while massaging his back, then finally how inviting her lips looked as they stood outside her van. "Yeah, I do."

"She may not stick."

"I'm aware." Cam closed the drawer on his toolbox and picked up his cut.

"Tracie is making pierogies and sausage tonight. Said to invite you for supper."

Cam put his arms through the holes and shifted the vest onto his shoulders. "I'm not on at the bar tonight, so that sounds good. I'm gonna run by my place and shower first. S'been a long day."

Quillon flicked two fingers at him as he turned and departed. "Don't wait too long. It's supposed to rain later."

Cam locked the door before heading to his bike. He was grateful that his boss didn't press any further. His feelings toward Sabrina were murky to himself at the moment. Yeah, he was drawn to her physically

—her body had all the right curves in all the right places—but it was more than that. Her gutsy attitude when they first met had lodged in his mind along with her story. How many women would be brave enough to uproot their entire lives and seek out life-changing answers? Sabrina struck him as having real courage to face such a challenge. It made her more attractive to him than any woman in a long time.

He wanted her. Check that: He wanted to get to know her better.

Would she let him in?

The bike underneath him purred but had no advice.

"Forget the past. Start over. Every day," Cam recited his personal motto, one that meant enough to him to permanently ink on his body.

It was time to live it.

10

Sabrina finished her last client of the day and stepped out of the room to let the older woman get dressed. She was a violinist in the Pittsburgh Symphony who had wrist and finger problems. Last week, the musician came to Sabrina to get her hands worked on. This week, she was back and had booked a regular time slot.

"I swear, you've made the biggest difference to my performances." The woman wiggled the stylus on the signature pad and added a generous tip. "I'm so glad I found you."

Sabrina smiled. "Thanks for that. See you next week?"

"For sure. Have a nice night!" she trilled as she walked out of the building.

This was the kind of client Sabrina enjoyed working with regularly—someone who needed her services and appreciated the help a good massage could bring. It almost made up for the two walk-ins Stephan had foisted on her earlier today. One was a woman who complained that her session was too rough, even after Sabrina had repeatedly asked her if the pressure was more than she wanted. The second was a man who let out a long "Ahh" as if climaxing every time she released a trigger point. He got so loud, she was afraid the other people in the spa would think something besides the man's back was getting a massage.

Sabrina's smile dropped with an exhausted sigh. It was Cicely's day off and Stephan had left early, leaving her to close up by herself. The days were getting dark earlier, and Sabrina didn't like riding her bike at night if she could help it. Cars were bad enough about messing with motorcyclists during the day, but it was always just a little worse after the sun went down.

No matter. She really didn't need to go anywhere, but sometimes it was nice to just ride. She and Ernie would do that after she got her first motorcycle. Rodrigo had his own bike but didn't like to use it much. Why he kept one was a mystery. Jealousy, perhaps?

The weekends riding over to Lido Key and hanging on the beaches with her dad were some of her best memories. Those were the times when she'd questioned nothing about her life, who she belonged to, and where her future lay. Her plans were to work at Amelia's place until she'd saved enough to open her own massage business.

When her world collapsed, she used a lot of her savings to purchase and outfit her van as a backup space until she got back on her feet. Pending that miracle, she still had to work and support herself, which brought her here to Pittsburgh to get some answers so she could restart her life.

For tonight, she could put all that aside and grab a quick shower. No other plans than snuggling up with Rugrat and Reptar, plus a good book. Food would be easy, as she had a stash of instant dinners she could grab from the break room freezer.

She locked the front door and walked down the hallway to the mudroom, where clients would get covered in a whole-body mud wrap for toning and cleansing. The tiled room had a handheld showerhead that hung over a central table. Cicely usually worked with those people, but Sabrina had helped a time or two. It was a small price to pay in order to use the facility after hours.

She pulled out the long braid she wore during the day and shook out her hair, letting the locks fall in thick waves around her face. Her eyes landed on the table with speculation. Yes, a mud wrap sounded nice, and she wasn't opposed to doing it on herself, but she was afraid she'd fall asleep and wake up in the morning to find herself in a crusty mess. Nope. Shower, then food, then book.

Her phone rang just as she gathered her bath items together from her locker. Rodrigo's name popped up, and she pursed her lips. She wished she could just delete his number, but the connection was necessary, at least for now. She pulled her lower lip between her teeth as she pondered answering, then, against her better judgment, swiped up.

"What do you want?"

"Your fucking signature on these papers."

The background noise told her there was a crowd at the house. Parties happened frequently after Rodrigo moved back into the family home, something Sabrina did not miss. The night one of her brother's buddies put his hands on her was the night she started living full-time in the converted van.

"Then bring your ass up here and I'll sign away."

"I can't just leave work."

Sabrina rolled her eyes. *Right, like no one else's job matters but yours.* "We've been through this already. Mail the damn things or send me a DocuSign email. I'll give you my work and personal email addresses. Take your pick."

"I don't trust that shit. You need to come down here."

Sabrina closed her locker door with a bang. "I don't have to do a goddamn thing. You and Aunt Rosa started this crap. Y'all can finish it."

"Why do you have to be such a bitch?"

She stopped in the hallway and let out a sarcastic laugh. "Bitch. Right. You threw me out of the family, and *I'm* the bitch."

"You were never family, *chica*. You were just a placeholder."

Rodrigo's nasty tone bit deeper than Sabrina was ready to hear. "Dad never felt that way, and you know it." She scoffed. "That's why you're being such a dick to me. It's 'cause Dad loved me no matter what, and you've always been jealous of that."

"Don't you talk about him like he was your *real* father! All you need to do is sign these papers and get the fuck out of my life."

"I already stated your options, *brother*. Ball's in your court now. Goodbye!"

Sabrina swiped the screen and resisted the urge to throw the device against the tile wall. Half a second later, she wiped angry tears from her eyes. "I can't believe I care enough to cry over this shit. Dad, why did you have to die?"

The walls had no answers.

Ernie was gone. Her family had abandoned her. She was in a strange city that didn't want her, with no real support from anyone, not even her work colleagues. She told herself it didn't matter and she could handle it.

It's rough when you can no longer believe your own lies.

Loneliness hit her hard. The tears kept falling, and no matter how many happy thoughts she tried to drum up, they didn't stop. She needed a shoulder, a hug, or just to hear the voice of another human who didn't hate her.

With trembling hands, she called the only person she trusted in Pittsburgh.

Cam parked his bike next to the van in the dark alley. The back door to the massage business was all but invisible in the dim light, the bulb over the opening doing nothing to dispel any shadows. Some light came from the van, but it was also limited by the curtains drawn over the window. If they were off, the van would disappear from sight. He had to admit, the likelihood of anyone coming back here to mess with his girl was low, given the visibility and isolation. Even so, he still despised the thought of her being here, alone and vulnerable.

He'd just finished eating at Quillon's place when he got the call from Sabrina. The tears were obvious in her voice, even though she was trying to hide them.

"Hi, Cam. Um... what are you doing tonight?"

"Having supper with my friends, then going home."

"Oh, okay. I was just thinking, maybe...."

Cam shifted the phone to his other ear as Quillon glanced at him with questioning eyes. "You okay, Sabrina?"

"Oh yeah, I'm just fine, sugar. I was just thinking, if you weren't busy...."

"You in your van?"

"Yes."

He didn't have to think about it. "I'm on my way."

Cam considered knocking or texting to tell her he was outside her door, but she must have noticed his arrival. The door slid open, and she waved him in with a smile. Her leggings were patterned in elephants, and her black tunic hung long and loose.

"Hey, sugar. You didn't have to come out here. I could have met you someplace for a drink or something."

"Supposed to rain soon. No one likes riding while you're getting pelted with water bullets."

She made a face. "Do you want to put your bike in the trailer just in case? It'll be a tight fit, but we can manage."

He wanted so badly to say, *"That's what she said,"* but he stopped himself. The mood wasn't right for joking. "Sure, thanks." He handed her a paper grocery bag. "Tracie sent this over. She thought you might not have eaten yet."

"What is it?"

"Sausage and pierogies."

She blinked. "Sausage is familiar and comes in several forms, but I've never heard of proggies."

"Pierogies. Potato dumplings. Tracie makes great ones, but not quite traditional. She sneaks bacon crumbles into hers."

Sabrina eyed the bag. "They sound interesting."

Cam smiled. "You got the trailer key handy? I'll get my bike settled before it starts coming down hard."

It took some effort, but he was able to get his bike into the trailer next to hers. Some bikers didn't worry about covering their rides for weather, but if shelter was available, he'd take it.

The van had more room in it than he thought. A small kitchenette area, folding table and bench on one side, and on the other…

"Holy shit! What are those?"

Sabrina laughed. "My kids, Rugrat and Reptar. They're bearded dragons. Want to meet them?"

Cam looked at the two lizards, the theme of her headgear suddenly making sense. "Why do you have them?"

"Presents from a former roommate. She moved out and left them behind. They're my roommates now. A lot cleaner and no complaints."

The two animals scurried to stare at him for a moment, as if sizing him up. One of them puffed up a bristled chin at him while the other crawled off to other parts of their enclosure. He and the lizard had a stare-off before the reptile gave up and moved to climb the tree.

He turned to see Sabrina sit at the table, open

the bag, and look at the plastic containers. Her laugh sounded genuine as she held one up. "I see people here do the same thing as Southern people—use Country Crock as Tupperware."

"My foster mom called them 'pass on' go-boxes. No need to return them, just use and pass on to the next person."

"I'll do what I can, but my storage is limited. You may get them back anyway." She pressed her fingers over one dish. "Oh, wow, it's still warm."

"Try one."

She fished out a pierogi with her fingers and bit into it. "This is soooo good!"

Her enjoyment pleased Cam. "Tracie is a great cook. I think you should meet her sometime."

"I'd love to. This beats the frozen Lean Cuisine I was planning on having tonight. Thank you."

A smattering of drops hit the roof, then increased until the sound blurred into one continuous sizzle. The noise didn't faze the lizards; they stayed curled up in their spots.

"Guess I'm not going anywhere for a while." Cam seated himself on the short padded bench next to Sabrina. "There's a couple chocolate cheesecake slices in there too. Tracie makes them with drizzle and chips on top. I thought since I didn't have supper with you, I'd at least do dessert."

Her eyes lit up at the word *cheesecake*. "Cam, you just became my favorite. Want a cup of coffee?"

"Sounds good to me."

She pulled down the small coffee maker and filled it from a half-empty five-gallon jug of water that sat in an alcove above the sink. A bowl of assorted pods came next. "Here, take your pick."

Cam fished out a Sumatra while Sabrina popped in a Colombian. Soon the gurgling sounds started, and a rich coffee aroma filled the van's interior.

"Thanks for coming to see me," she said. "You really didn't have to. I've survived worse things than being alone."

He watched her fill her mug with the potent brew and prep for a second cup. "It's not a problem. You sounded like you needed company, and I'm not at work for a change." As the rain picked up in volume, his brain gave him a brilliant idea. "Since we're gonna be stuck with each other for a while, wanna play a game?"

She pulled two forks from a drawer. "Sure. What game?"

"Truth or dare."

She stopped and smiled. "Really? We used to play that in high school a bazillion years ago."

"I'm feeling nostalgic."

"Cream and sugar, sugar?"

"Black."

She doctored hers before sitting back down on the bench. "Okay, I'll start. Truth or dare?"

"Truth."

"You said something about a foster mom earlier."

Cam took a big sip of the coffee and forked up a bite of cheesecake. "I met Vera when I was nine. She and her husband, Cecil, never had kids of their own. They just took care of others. There were four of us: Tammie, Kyle, Morgan, and me. They were more like foster grandparents, but they were the best. Your turn. Truth or dare?"

"Truth."

"Why did you really call me tonight?"

Sabrina's smile dimmed a little. "It was kind of a shitty day. I had a couple walk-ins who didn't like my work very much. Before that, the last new client I got stuck with had trouble keeping his hands to himself, and he threatened to leave a bad review. Cicely didn't have my back when she found out." She twirled the fork in the top of her cheesecake. "Normally, I wouldn't take that kind of shit, but I need this job. It also didn't help that my asshole stepbrother is on my case about something too. All of that piled on me enough to make me want to see a friendly face, so I called you."

Cam's blood rose. "Say that again? Someone put their hands on you?"

He watched as Sabrina licked chocolate from the tines of her fork. "It's not that. I've had that happen before, and truthfully, it's not that frequent, but it is annoying. No, it was that my boss was more upset over a potential bad review than clients disrespecting her employees."

Cam did not like that, neither the client nor the boss.

When he looked at her again, the motion of her tongue as it searched for the chocolate drizzle made heat erupt in his belly, which rivaled the building anger in his head. "Someone ever fucks with you again, you call me, yeah?"

Her quizzical eyes met his. "Why? I can handle myself, Cam."

"You shouldn't have to handle anything. At least not alone." He cleared his throat in an attempt to cool off a bit. "What about your brother?"

She picked up a big chunk of the crust. "Stepbrother. I talked to him earlier. He's been hounding me to go back to Florida and sign a bunch of papers that have something to do with Dad's estate. He died without a will in place. I don't know how probate works, but I guess it's something to do with proving legitimacy. Rodrigo was legally adopted, so he's supposed to inherit, but if I'm Ernie's blood relative, he'll have to split it with me." She shook her head. "After all the crap he put me through, I don't feel obligated to help him."

Cam's temper rose a few more degrees, outpacing his libido for the moment. "The post office still exists."

She sighed and bit into the graham cracker sweetness. "He said he doesn't trust the mail. This is really good."

"Like I said, Tracie is a great cook. So, you need me to go to Florida and kick some ass?"

"I'll think about it," she told him with a sassy grin. She lowered her eyes and took another bite of the dessert. "Truth or dare?"

Cam recognized a dismissal when he heard one. It bothered him. A lot. He reached over to put his coffee cup in the sink. "Truth."

"How many girlfriends have you had?"

Shit! That was a question he didn't want to answer. "Positive you want to hear this?"

She settled back into a big throw pillow that doubled as a cushion and brought her bent legs up. The tight space forced her bare feet to rest just on his thigh. The contact was casual, yet he felt every bit of it. "Yes, actually. I'm curious."

Cam took the other pillow and put it behind his back. "I've been with more women than I want to admit, dated a few, but only one actual girlfriend. We stopped seeing each other after high school."

"Why did you break up?"

"Long story."

"Wanna tell me?"

"No." His abrupt answer made the corners of her mouth turn down. He didn't like seeing that, but he wasn't ready for that level of sharing. Some things in his past needed to stay there. "Truth or dare?"

"Truth."

"Same question. How many boyfriends have *you* had?"

She raised an eyebrow and reached out a bare foot to tap the top of his thigh. His dick twitched in response. "Only two, and one of them was in high school. I can count on one hand the number of lovers I've had and still have fingers left over." She pursed her lips. "Truth or dare?"

He grabbed the foot that pushed against his leg.

This slow dance was headed toward the danger zone. It was time to step it up a little. "Dare."

The air in the van changed. A subtle tension ramped up his back as he waited for her challenge. He had a notion what it would be and hoped he was right.

"I dare you to kiss me."

The invitation was there, and he took it. Without hesitation, he moved in and covered her mouth with his, tasting coffee and chocolate. She kissed him back, opening for him. It turned into an unhurried exploration of tongues, teeth, and lips. A slow burn started in his belly, one that resembled the heating of a billet. Metal had stages of color when it was annealed in a furnace: gray to blue to black to dark red to bright cherry to orange. It took time to reach each level, and once it did, it could become anything. Any form he wished to make.

What they would forge between them had yet to be decided, but the furnace had lit up.

The kiss ended. Cam found himself on top of Sabrina with one leg on the floor and the other between her thighs, his mouth hovering over hers. Tension and need permeated the air along with uncertainty. They'd reached a turning point, and neither of them wanted to make the next move.

Sabrina licked her lips as if tasting Cam's flavor. "It's still raining."

It was indeed. The heavy downpour still pounded the van, and it didn't sound like it would let up anytime soon.

"Do you want me to leave?" he asked in a rough voice.

"No."

"What *do* you want, Sabrina?" He was sure she could feel his heavy groin through their clothes. Only a couple of layers lay between them. If they were naked, he'd be inside her already—if she wanted that to happen. Her kiss dare made him think she did.

She took a few deep breaths, as if calming herself into control. "I'm not a slut. I don't sleep around or do one-nighters. But right now… I think I need you."

"I think I need you." Those words burned themselves into his mind and his gut like an iron brand. But as much as he wanted to, the timing wasn't right. Forging a blade took many steps, patience, and methodical work. Skipping ahead left the metal too soft to hold an edge or too brittle to last. If he wanted whatever this was to be long and solid, he needed to get the tempering right.

Cam spoke in a rough voice. "I'm not fucking you

tonight. I'm not fucking you ever. When we get together, and we will, it will be more than just scratching an itch. We'll be 100 percent sure we're ready for that step, 'cause once we take it, there's no going back."

She licked her lips. For several moments, they stayed frozen, the air heavy and thick, neither one moving forward or backward or breaking. Cam held himself rigid, wondering how long they could listen to the storm without falling prey to its power and giving in. He could see himself kissing her hard, testing her response, and pushing her to open up and take him inside. His erection screamed for relief; only his iron will kept him still.

"I have a flat-screen over my bed so I can stream movies when I get a chance to hook into a Wi-Fi signal," she finally said, but her eyes never moved from his.

Apparently, they weren't going to talk about it. Very well, he would play the game and sweep everything under the rug. For now.

"I can do a movie."

11

Garfield Hob opened the door to his shop and entered the dim interior. *"People needs good shoes, and good shoes needs repair"* was a phrase often repeated by his father. After Garfield Senior passed away, Garfield Junior expanded into repairing baseball gloves, purses, and belts. Some days he was a cobbler, and other days he was a leathersmith. Either way, the shop maintained a steady flow of customers.

The sweet, earthy smell of conditioning oils wafted through the open door. He inhaled the familiar scent. He'd been working in this shop since he was seven, and thirty years later, he was still at it.

Garfield pulled down the leather apron from its hook and replaced it with his jacket. Mornings were cold, but the afternoon should warm up a bit. He opened the plastic grocery bag his wife handed him an hour ago. Two chipped ham sandwiches, a can of cheddar cheese Pringles, a cup of fruit cocktail, and a big brownie. He smiled as he put his lunch in the small fridge. They were coming up on ten years married with two children, and every morning she sent him to work with a similar packed lunch. He felt so lucky to have this beautiful life.

Shelves with pairs of customers' work shoes, boots, and belts lined one side of the shop, but the majority of the space was taken up by the working area. Garfield's main bench held several shoe anvils and had an array of leather working tools hanging from the pegboard at the back. Awls, knives, leather scissors, rotary cutters, thread, and assorted shaping tuckers lay close to his hands when he needed them. Several rows of lasts, otherwise known as shoe forms, sat in a regimented row across the shelf at the top of his workbench. He didn't do as much custom work as his father had, but they were still a part of the shop and his heritage.

Most of these tools had been here for decades, the handles well-worn and dark with age. The same awls he'd learned to poke through the leather to sew soles were the same ones he used now. He loved his craft, and it was getting rarer to find someone with these skills. He wondered if his six-year-old son would eventually carry on the tradition.

Garfield checked the day's scheduled workload before starting the coffee maker. *"No work begins until coffee is made"* was another phrase his father was fond of saying. As the water bubbled through the filter, he picked up one of the knives and tested the blade. It was time to make a run to Quillon's place and have it sharpened. The machine shop was only a block away on the next row of businesses after the titty bar. But even that close, he would have to make a trip after hours or have Mira watch the shop for him while the kids were in school. Sharpening was one skill he'd never quite mastered. He could do some maintenance, but when it came to a good edge, Quillon had a guy working there who was a genius at making blades.

Garfield pulled out a pair of shoes with worn soles and set up to get started. He poured his coffee before setting one shoe over the anvil.

A moment later, he heard the door open behind him, and he frowned. His first appointment wasn't until nine. He started to turn.

"Can I help—"

Pain exploded across the back of his skull. His

legs suddenly gave out, and he hit the floor with a bang. More pain hit his ribs, and he felt one snap. Confusion steeped with fear flooded his mind.

Why?

The last thing he saw was a brown puddle of coffee and a broken mug that said "World's Best Dad."

12

Cam sat at his spot at one of the round tables and flipped a pen around his thumb. Wolf had called this meeting via text, and most of the Knights were present. Only two customers sat at the bar, drinking their lunch and staring at Ellie's naked tits as she did her thing at the pole. When the men finally looked away and spotted the gathering of bikers, they quickly decided they were done for the day. Ellie pouted at the lost tips.

"Cheapskates!" she declared as she scampered off the stage. Her breasts bounced as she stomped angrily to the small dressing room in the back.

He noticed Ratchet staring at her retreating ass with a speculative look. Ellie was a bit of a ditz, but she could take care of herself. If Ratchet wanted to make a move, it was up to her to say yes or no.

Cam's mind was more on Sabrina and the events from last night than the meeting. The nasty storm had turned into a long, soaking rain that lasted for several hours. He didn't remember the movie ending. It was some thriller with a zombie virus. The film wasn't memorable, but the time with Sabrina had stayed with him. Surprisingly, the bed fit them both and was comfortable as hell. He'd lain on his back against the thick pillows, and she had curled into his side. The movie played out on the screen, but he didn't hear it. His attention was on the warm presence next to him.

Her breathing.

Her scent.

Her touch.

The noises she made as she fell asleep.

When the sun rose and bathed them in light from the small roof window, he woke to find himself in the same position. They'd stayed fully clothed, and neither of them had tried anything more than the kiss she'd dared him to take, but he felt more satisfied and rested than if he'd had a sex marathon. It had been years since he slept with a woman until morning.

He wondered when they could do it again.

His attention turned quickly as Wolf cracked a newly made gavel onto a round bench anvil. Quillon had turned it on one of the lathes last week, complaining about getting wood chips mixed up with the metal ones.

Wolf didn't care. Anyone who saw his face at that moment could tell he was pissed. "Three hits to the neighborhood. First the coffee shop, then Clauson's, and now Hob's shoe place. This shit has to stop."

Melter reached for his joint-making apparatus and thought better of it. "The coffee shop people are gay. Someone might have hit them because of that."

The table erupted in grumbles. Yes, gay businesses were regular targets for some hate groups, but the Knights weren't that kind of club.

"Nah," Baghouse scoffed. "The other places had the same attacks. Broken shit and Molotov cocktails. Al and Edna never hurt anyone. The only reason Clauson's didn't burn to the ground was 'cause old Al had a good sprinkler system installed. The shoe place was saved 'cause Specs saw Garfield gettin' beat up and called the police. The perps didn't have time to bomb the place."

A smattering round of applause popped around the tables, and Specs grinned at the recognition.

"Damn lucky you were around." Quillon reached out to slap Specs on the shoulder. The smaller man grimaced and grinned at the same time. "How's Garfield doin'?"

Wolf dropped the gavel onto the table with a clatter. "He's in critical condition and alive for now, but it's not looking good. Serious concussion. Broken arm. Bruised and broken ribs, one punctured lung. Docs say he may or may not make it. If he does, he's gonna be out of work with a shit ton of hospital bills."

"Tracie visited his wife and kids yesterday. Money is tight. Garfield's the only breadwinner. Mira doesn't work and stays home with the kids. One of them is in school, but the daycare for the other kid would cost them more than what she would earn. Not worth it for her to get a job."

Melter made a tsking noise. "Dude, that sucks."

Specs cleared his throat. "If they need help, maybe we could...." His voice trailed off as he realized all the eyes in the room were on him.

"Spit it out," Wolf gruffed.

Specs tried again. "I was just thinking that maybe we could... like...."

"Like what?"

"Like hold a charity rally or something like that."

Baghouse barked out a short laugh. "What kinda stupid idea is that, ya damn jagoff?"

A streak of anger traveled down Cam's spine. "You got any better ones?"

Wolf pursed his lips, seeming to consider it. "No one's been to a rally in a long time. We've never held one before either."

Cam let out a long breath. "It's a lot of work to put one together," he admitted.

"It wouldn't have to be big like Sturgis," Wolf put in. "Just local folks helping local folks. Might be a good way to let everyone know about the vandalism and to keep vigilant."

"I think it's a good idea," Quillon added. "Tracie is good at organizing shit. She can help Specs get that together. The question is when?"

Cam put the pen in his hand down on the table. "A community rally sounds cool, but if we're gonna do it, we need to do it quick. The weather's getting colder, and it's unpredictable."

Wolf put his elbows on the table and dangled the gavel in his hands. "Since we're talking just local people, let's say two weeks on Saturday. Would that work? I'll ask Jazz to pitch in for the graphics and advertising. She knows more about social media than I do."

Melter rubbed an open palm over his face. "Shit, it's fucking hot in here. Hey, Specs, go in the back and turn the heat off, yeah? Fucking weather can't tell if it's still summer or fall."

The smaller man nodded and scampered to the rear of the building as Melter continued his tirade. "Yo, how does a fucking rally help with the fucking attacks?"

Cam noted the biker's shaking hand but kept his mouth shut. He'd seen withdrawal before. Everyone in the club knew about Melter's pot habit. The question was what else the biker might be using. He put aside that speculation, as it was none of his business and there were other priorities at the moment. "We should think again about patrols. We can't cover everything, but riding at night in pairs might help. If it stops just one hit, it's worth the gas money."

Baghouse gave another irritated huff. "How the hell is a random ride gonna help?"

"Not random," Quillon said with a serious air. "Every one of those businesses is a place we go to. I go to the coffee shop almost every morning. So does Tracie. We all use Clauson's store, and several of us at the machine shop have Garfield repair our work boots. This is targeted."

Baghouse wouldn't let it go. "You're out of your mind."

"Am I? I hope so. All's I'm saying is, if we put the places we're associated with on some sort of route, we might catch these assholes faster."

Wolf set the gavel on the table and leaned back. "At least it's a plan. Worst-case, it doesn't work." He shifted uncomfortably. The padded chairs were reserved for Scrap and Baghouse. The rest were hard wood seats and weren't made for long sitting times. "Quillon, make up a schedule, yeah?"

"You bet."

"Anybody think the Slaggers MC might be back?" This came from Crossman. He seldom spoke in these meetings, but when he did, he usually had something worth hearing.

"I doubt it," Cam replied. "Something would have buzzed down the grapevine by now if they were reforming."

Wolf grunted. "Without Ramrod, they have no leader to pull them back together."

Specs came back into the room and resumed his spot. "That's not what I heard."

All eyes rocketed to the newest member. The smaller man squirmed as the entire club waited to hear more. "Um... I just... like rumors about their colors being seen around again, ya know?" he spluttered. "I don't know if it's real or not. Just rumors."

Wolf picked up the gavel again. "We'll stick with our plan. Specs, since you had the rally idea, find us a place to hold it other than in front of the bar. We need a family vibe, not one that includes naked titties."

Specs preened a little and did his quirky salute. "Aye-aye, captain!"

"Good." Wolf raised the gavel and cracked it on the table. "Dismissed."

"I think you're supposed to say 'adjourned.'"

Wolf rolled his eyes. "Whatever. Go do whatever the fuck you're supposed to be doing at this hour."

Cam picked up his cut but didn't bother putting it on. The machine shop sat next door on the other side of Attic and extended to the corner, with a parking lot adjacent to the strip of buildings where both patrons and customers parked either during the day or night. There was a gravel spot just behind the machine shop that Sabrina's rig would fit into nicely. He hoped like hell she would take him up on his offer and move to this side of the neighborhood. The spa was only about a ten-minute ride from here, but a lot of shit could happen in that time.

"Hold up a sec, Cam," Wolf called out as he

stood up and rubbed his ass. "Damn hard seats. I wanted to update you on Scrap. I went by his house this morning to check on him. His recovery isn't goin' well, even though he won't say shit about it. Thought you'd want to know so you can tell your girl."

Cam didn't have to guess who Wolf referred to. "Yeah, I'll let her know." He paused. "Think that old goat will ever take the DNA test and give Sabrina the answer she needs?"

Wolf sighed. "Both of them need those answers, so I hope he does. I'll talk to him about it when I deliver the news about the rally idea." He gave Cam a speculative look. "What happens next? If Scrap isn't her father, is she gonna pull up stakes and go somewhere else? If he *is* her father, will she put down roots?"

Cam shook his head. "I have no idea. This living-in-limbo shit would drive me crazy."

"Yeah, me too."

"I gotta get over to the shop. There's a bunch of one-off orders to fill, and we're already behind."

Wolf nodded. "I'll see you tonight. Get some sleep if you can. It might be a long one."

13

Sabrina dumped a load of sheets into the washer and added detergent. If there was time between clients, everyone took turns keeping up with laundry and other tasks around the spa. Stocking oils, making calls, cleaning bathrooms—whatever task was needed, the expectation was for the staff to jump in and get it done.

Stephan walked by the open laundry room, playing a game on his phone.

Sabrina called out to him, "Hey, Steph, can you check the mudroom for any towels?"

The man actually looked down his nose at her. "Really? I don't do menial." He walked off with the sounds of *Mario Kart* following him.

It pissed her off, but she reminded herself that this place was just a temporary gig until she figured out what came next.

She closed the machine lid and turned the dial to start it.

What *did* come next?

Up until last night, she had a plan, but the impulsive dare threw her off. What possessed her to ask for that kiss? Now she couldn't stop thinking about it.

When was the last time she did that? Years ago, when she and Carlos had their thing going. They'd been high school sweethearts. He was her first kiss and first big crush. She gave her virginity to him at graduation, and they'd dated a little while longer after that, but he had other plans that included four years of football at the University of Georgia. Those plans didn't include her. Later, there was Parker, but his love was based on her breadwinning capabilities. Right off the bat, he'd tried to move in with her and suggested he become a house-boyfriend. Nope. Whoever she lived with didn't have to support her, but he damn well needed to support himself. Ernie taught her that.

"If a man can't stand on his own two feet, you don't need him."

Sabrina paused as she recalled her dad's words. She had to thank her on-again, off-again mother for that as well. Raquel spent most of her life sponging off any man she could find to give her money. Sabrina vowed a long time ago to never be that kind of woman.

"Find something you like that you can earn your own living doing, mija. Always be able to pay your own bills and take care of yourself."

That's exactly what she did. Ernie had helped her out as much as he could with school, but she'd paid most of her own way and made it into a career. In the short time she'd been here in Pittsburgh, she'd met a number of people and built a budding reputation. More musicians were coming to see her about hand and elbow issues, and a few of them offered comp tickets for any concerts she wanted to see.

Would Cam be interested in hearing the symphony?

She closed her eyes and took a cleansing breath. *Stop thinking about him all the damn time!*

The vision of this morning appeared behind her eyelids. Waking up, seeing his handsome face relaxed as he slept on, his arm around her as he held her close and secure. All of it was etched into her memory, and she would never forget the sense of safety she felt, of belonging.

She took another breath, drawing air deep into her lungs, and held it. *Stop it, Sabrina. You're too old to have schoolgirl crushes anymore.*

The pep talk didn't work.

Stephan broke her concentration by calling her from the front.

"Earth to Sabrina! You have a new person up in here!"

She gritted her teeth. Her next appointment was in two hours, so this must be a walk-in type or someone Stephan didn't want to deal with. *Money is money,* she thought as she walked down the hall to the counter.

The short, tubby man wore a business suit that was at least one size too small. He drove a hand through his spiked-up hair, lifting it farther as he snapped irritably, "No, no, no, no! I said two hundred twenty-four, not twenty-four hundred!"

Sabrina's confusion dissipated when she spotted the dual Bluetooth devices in his ears.

"Absolute incompetence! Someone's getting fired. I'll give you an hour to figure out who. What's taking so long?"

A moment passed before Sabrina realized he was talking to her. "I'm ready when you are. Right this way."

The man punched at his ear and stomped down the hall like a steaming bull. Sabrina's radar pinged that this session would not be fun. She followed him and pointed him to her room. "I'll give you a minute to get undressed, okay?"

The grunt she got in return was not reassuring.

Fuck, this is going to be tough. Cicely said no bad reviews, and you need this job. Don't cuss him, don't cuss him, don't cuss him....

Her internal monologue wasn't convincing either. After waiting a couple of minutes, she took a long, cleansing breath and knocked before entering the small studio.

The smell hit her first. He lay face down on the table, exuding a combination of sweat, sour, and shit. This guy stank like he hadn't bathed or used deodorant in a while.

You're kidding me. I gotta work on him? No wonder Stephan handed him over to me.

Sabrina put a hand over her nose. The time she'd worked on Cam directly from the machine shop, he admitted to being smelly, but he wasn't this bad. He was clean under his sweat, so to speak, and used hygiene products. His scent had been a combination of machine oil, Speed Stick, and man—not unpleasant, at least to her. The man currently on her table was unwashed and sour.

There was a lavender-scented candle in her room on the utility table in the corner. She moved to light it in an attempt to mask the pungent odor, but the guy interrupted her.

"Don't light that shit. I hate smelly candles."

I hate smelly jerks! she thought right back at him. Somehow, she managed to nod and smile, but her eyes began to water. Breathing through her mouth wasn't an option either, as she could almost taste the stink.

"You just gonna stand there, or do I get my gawddamn massage?"

Good Lord in heaven, please get me through this session without losing my job for smackin' this asshole!

"Are there any places that you want me to work on specifically?"

"My back hurts, and my feet are crampin' like crazy."

Oh shit! Do I have to touch his feet?

Sabrina debated the merits of pulling the fire alarm just outside the room door as she strapped an oil dispenser to her hip. She did not want to put her hands on this man. Just the thought was making her gag a bit. "Okay. Let me know if the pressure is too much."

The man's fleshy back was covered in red patches of some sort of dermatitis. Rather than risk herself, Sabrina quickly pulled a pair of nitrile medical gloves from a supply drawer. Using gloves was not her favorite, but her choices were to refuse the massage or risk losing her job. The oil she pulled out had antibacterial properties in it, so she reasoned she should be protected enough to complete this odious task.

Once she started, she realized his back was full of crunchy tight spots. The moment she dug into one, he cussed and hollered at her. "That fuckin' hurts!"

Sabrina gritted her teeth. "I'm sorry. I'll lighten up the pressure."

"Moron." He uttered the word softly, but she still heard it.

Don't cuss him, don't cuss him, don't cuss him.... She added more oil to her hands. "Is that any better?"

"Can you just do your job and not talk?"

A flare of anger made her want to jab the guy's ribs in a painful trigger point, but she reasoned that maybe if she didn't speak, the smell might get easier to handle.

Not thirty seconds later, he yanked up his arm, nearly knocking her over, and jabbed at his ear. "Yeah?"

Sabrina stopped working on his shoulder as he started yelling.

"What the fuck, Tony? Get your fuckin' ass over to the shipping department pronto and tell them to get it done."

Whatever Tony said set the guy off even more. He jerked himself up and planted his elbows on the table as he continued to lose his mind. "What do you mean, there's not enough time? We got a three o'clock deadline to make! This is your fuckup, pal! What's your problem?"

Again, it took a moment for Sabrina to figure out he'd switched people and was talking to her now. She pulled the last ice cube of patience from the bottom of her glass. "I don't have a problem. I'm just waiting for you to conclude your business so I can continue."

"Look, cupcake, I don't wanna rain on your parade, but when I pay for a gawddamn massage, I expect to get a gawddamn massage!"

From the word *cupcake*, all bets were off. "You

want a 'gawddamn' massage? I'll give you the best 'gawddamn' massage you've ever had. Just do the world a favor and shower the shit stink off your ass first. You smell like you dropped a load and didn't clean up after."

The man stared at her in stunned silence, his red, pudgy face falling as slack as his protruding belly that squished out on either side of his body. "Did you just speak to me like that?"

Fuck this job! If Cicely doesn't support me in this, I'm outta here anyway, so I've got nothing to lose.

Sabrina didn't hesitate. "Yes, I did. You've been a totally disrespectful asshat since you walked in here. I'm wasting my time working on you because you're fighting me. You're rude as fuck, and you smell so bad I want to puke!"

"I can't help it if I got no time for a shower this morning! I sweat a lot!"

"Then don't get a massage until you *do* bathe!"

The man spluttered something about her being unprofessional and that she should be fired, but Sabrina didn't hear him as she walked out of the room and slammed the door behind her.

Cicely came out of the mudroom. "What's going on? Who's yelling?"

"Mr. Shitty Diaper in there." Sabrina flicked a

hand at her room. "I don't know what your policy is on working with people who have poor hygiene or questionable skin conditions or ones who are just plain assholes, but I'm not dealing with that shit. If you want to fire me, go ahead."

She turned to see Stephan standing in the doorway leading to the front counter. The man had his arms crossed and a shit-eating smirk on his face. Sabrina raised her middle finger at him as she stormed out. "Fuck you!"

The cold air cooled her temper, and she slowed her pace. She didn't know where her feet were taking her, but she kept going. At least her phone was in her pocket, so she wasn't without any resources.

Who would she call? In retrospect, she couldn't afford to lose this job, but at the same time, there was only so much crap she could take. An aesthetician told her this spa had a revolving door for employees. No one stayed there very long either because of pay or the general work environment, or both. She could definitely see why. And while Sabrina was grateful for the opportunity and the leeway with parking her van out back, that didn't mean anyone had the right to walk all over her.

Worry hit her that Stephan or Cicely would call

someone to tow her van and trailer. "Dammit!" she muttered. "If I have to apologize to that guy.... Nope, I can't do it."

She had the option of returning to her previous route between Planet Fitness and Walmart parking lots at least for now. Then she paused. Why the hell was she even sticking around? It was clear Scrap wasn't going to give her any answers. Even though she was low on funds, she wasn't flat busted broke. She hadn't put down roots in this city. Nothing was stopping her from loading up her van and taking off. Maybe that was for the best.

She thought briefly about Cam and how he would take the news of her leaving. Regret pierced her heart as she thought about not seeing him again. Last night had the potential of turning into something special, but today....

She turned around, intending to call the spa to officially quit, but she heard someone calling her.

"Sabrina!"

She spotted the person who'd embedded himself in her life and didn't seem to want to go. Cam approached her, walking stiffly.

Those psoas muscles are giving him trouble again.

"Hey, Cam."

He stopped in front of her. "Everything okay?"

Not really. "Yeah, everything is fine. I forgot to ask if Scrap made it home from the hospital."

"He did, and Wolf checked on him this morning. What's wrong?"

His face showed such concern that for a moment, she wanted to do nothing more than cry. "Nothing's wrong. I was just asking."

"Then why are you here looking like someone stole Reptar and Rugrat instead of at work?"

"No one is gonna steal my babies. I just needed some fresh air. The last client I had smelled like ass and acted like one too."

"Long ways to walk. 'Bout a half mile from here to the spa." His demeanor changed from concern to anger in a heartbeat. "Did this ass touch you or say something to you?"

Tears welled in her eyes, but she didn't let them fall. Not yet. When was the last time anyone had this kind of concern for her? Definitely not since Ernie passed away. Her dad always figured out when she was down and often took her for ice cream. He had a manner of calmly talking to her and asking questions until she finally opened up and told him what bothered her. The closest person she had now was Amelia, and even then, there were limits.

"I'm just having another really shitty day, that's all."

To her surprise, he stepped forward and folded her into his body, tucking her head into the space between his neck and shoulder.

"I'm sorry, babe. Tell me how I can make it better."

She sighed as his warmth penetrated her shirt. She hadn't realized she was cold until he surrounded her. "I think you're doing it already." Another sigh passed her lips. "I cussed the asshole out and left in the middle of a job. Cicely told me she would fire me if I made her have another bad review. I expect that's what's about to happen when I go get my rig."

"We'll give her some very positive ones. Wolf needs his back done, and there's others in the club who need your services. Watch out for Melter, though. He's unpredictable."

Somewhere above, she heard him chuckle. "Of course, the operative syllable in that word is *dick*. Best just to stay away from him."

His heart beat in a steady rhythm below her ear. The heavy sensation of his arms around her body felt like a shield she could hide behind forever. A couple of cars passed by on the busy street, and someone shouted in the distance, but nothing penetrated the wall of protection he offered. It was comfortable, and Sabrina found she wanted all that and more. "I will."

"I have to work at the club tonight. In the morning, I'll help you move your rig."

She didn't even think about protesting. "Sounds good to me."

He pulled back and gazed deep into her eyes. His were also a shade of blue, though more on the charcoal side. She noticed the dark ring surrounding his irises as his fingertips moved to lift her chin. His mouth descended and covered hers in a slow, burning kiss that reminded her of last night. No ton of bricks fell on her, no electric flash traveling through her body. Just a smoldering that filled her belly with the promise of more heat to come.

He finally raised his head, and his breath brushed over her lips.

"Where is this going?" she asked in a quivery whisper.

"I don't know, babe, but I'm not ready to stop."

"Me neither."

He released her and cleared his throat. "You can sit in the break room and look through the want ads for another spa opening."

"No need for that."

Both of them jumped at the amused voice. Wolf stepped up to join them on the sidewalk. "I just called to book an appointment with Sabrina and expressed my disappointment that she wasn't there because the Knights plan to make her our official masseuse." The big man's face split into a grin. "I also mentioned our rally and how we would support all our sponsors. She's got a check waiting for me. I think your job is safe. If Cam's okay with it, I'll take you back to the spa now if you want to work on me."

Sabrina smiled and stepped back, putting some distance between her and Cam. Relief coursed through her body, mixed with a little humility. The Knights didn't have to go to bat for her, but they did, and it made her a little nervous. Not many people stood up for her, and she wasn't sure how to handle it. *Fuck it, I'll take the win.* "I'll do you anytime. Massage, that is."

Wolf tossed his head back and let out a huge belly laugh.

Cam frowned at his friend's amusement and turned his attention back to Sabrina. "That's cool, but I still want you to move tomorrow morning. I'm sure getting that van and trailer back there wasn't easy. It's going to be even harder to get it out."

She blinked. "Okay, sugar."

"I'll get whoever is available to come spot. Those suckers are tricky as hell to maneuver. Might need to move the trailer separate. Where's it going?" Wolf asked.

Cam answered before Sabrina could open her mouth. "My place."

14

Brianna Fletcher heaved a big box of paperbacks from the floor to one of the reading tables, then flopped down into the fluffy wingback chair to catch her breath. The used bookstore and tea shop fulfilled her dream of owning a business that filled both passions in her life, reading and sipping tea. Having it a couple of doors down from the spa was a bonus. It was the perfect location, as people going to and coming from Cicely's place often stopped in for a cup and a browse.

The downside of the bookstore was running the place by herself. No vacations or time off. She was open six days a week from nine to seven and never closed on holidays. Her mom stayed in a perpetual state of irritation at her since she missed services regularly.

"How you gonna find a good man, missing church all the time?"

"You gotta put more effort in than other girls. Do yourself up, right?"

"You should look into some cosmetic surgery, n'at. It'd be a good thing to fix your nose, yeah?"

Bri was acutely aware that she was not even remotely pretty, and the daily reminders from her mother were all the more reason to stay away from her parents.

It was well past closing time. Most of the other businesses had already shuttered their doors for the day, but she often stayed after hours simply to catch up on paperwork and restock. People came to trade their books, but this was the only time she could go through any boxes and check on titles. The shelves were mostly full of romantic fiction, but there were sections for crafting, self-help, religion, travel, and other genres. Just yesterday, a cute guy in a leather vest came in to look for a book on chain mail. She had three, and he bought them all.

Bri suppressed a grin. He talked with her for a long time about armor and metals and medieval knight stuff. His smile was contagious, and she found herself opening up to him about her love of fantasy. After he left, she had to shake herself silly to dispel any notion that he might be interested in her.

Not gonna happen, Bri.

She opened the top of the box and started pulling out books, piling them into stacks according to type. The majority were cookbooks, and one caught her eye about baking different homemade breads.

"This one might have to come home with me," she muttered as she licked her thumb to page through the recipes. Perhaps she could start baking tea buns or scones to sell. Wouldn't that be fun? Expanding the tea shop would be cool too.

Her head was full of the future when something crashed through her window. She had a split second to look up before flames erupted on the front shelves.

"Oh no!" she cried, dropping the bread book.

She lunged at the small fire extinguisher behind the front counter. In the few seconds it took for her to figure out how to operate the device, the fire had spread to three other stacks. The books acted like a smorgasbord of fuel. Bri sprayed a pitifully small stream toward the flames, but it petered out quickly, leaving nothing to stop the growing inferno.

I have to get out!

Her head swiveled between the front of the store and the back. The raging fire blocked both. She coughed as acrid smoke entered her lungs. Vaguely remembering something about fire safety, she fell to the floor, but it wasn't enough. She gagged as she crawled, trying to make her brain work.

The crash of the front door giving way startled her, and she raised her burning eyes to see a man in a black vest rushing in. A bandana covered his nose and mouth, but she recognized him as the guy who came in for the chain mail books.

"Help me," she tried to cry out, but it only came out as a whisper before a fit of coughing took away any voice she had left.

He grasped her arms and yanked her up with bruising force. She didn't care as long as they got out of this madness. Flames licked at both of them as he half dragged her to the door. Once outside, he continued to pull her farther into the street. She collapsed into several other pairs of arms as she gagged and coughed, desperate to get any air into her lungs.

"I got her, Crossman. You can let go."

The words reached her as if resonating from the

bottom of a deep well. She was still alive, but her store was toast. Literally.

If she could cry then and there, she would have. All the work, money, and time she'd invested had gone up in smoke within minutes. She would grieve it later when she could breathe again, but a simple one-word question remained in her mind.

Why?

THE SIRENS WOKE SABRINA FROM A DEEP SLEEP. She sat up from the nest of blankets on her bed and rubbed her eyes awake. The dark was absolute, and she fumbled to find the battery-powered reading lamp above her head.

"What the hell?" she muttered.

The piercing blare got closer, and fear bloomed in her chest. *There's a fire, and it's close.* She sniffed the air but smelled nothing more than the lavender spray she used on her pillow.

The noise grew louder, then stopped like the big trucks were right outside her windows. She reached out to pull one of the coverings down to check outside her vehicle, but something made her pause. Whatever instinct kicked in told her there was something out there in the alley with her. Something she needed to leave alone.

If she lifted that cover, not only would she see whatever was out there, but it would see her too.

With trembling fingers, she clicked the lamp back off and wrapped herself in the blankets. The van was locked, but she still felt vulnerable as she huddled in her bed. Rugrat or Reptar skittered across the enclosure as she strained her ears to hear something. Anything.

More emergency sirens filtered in from the front street. Something had happened. She had no clue what it was, but it sounded bad if that many emergency vehicles showed up. Maybe she needed to move her rig now, but that meant she would have to remove the front blackout covering.

Her eyes cut to the driver's windshield. *Stop being so dramatic! There's nothing out there.* But she still couldn't make herself move. There sat a malevolence just beyond that curtain. Whether physical or her imagination, it paralyzed her into silence. Her senses stayed hyper-focused as the minutes passed.

A sudden pounding on the door made her scream and fall off the bed.

"Sabrina! It's me. Open up!" Cam's demanding voice shouted.

The Gordian knot in her stomach broke apart, and she sobbed lightly in relief. "Hold your horses, sugar."

She unlocked the door and let him in.

"There's a fire a couple doors down. Bookstore. Total loss." His face was streaked with soot and grime. "We're not waiting 'til daylight. We're moving you now."

15

The air at the church meeting changed. Gone were the lackadaisical attitudes and apathetic looks. The Knights were on full alert as they sat around their tables. Wolf banged the gavel once, but the room was already quiet, everyone waiting to hear the latest news.

"Yinz heard about the bookstore last night. Bri is in the hospital. Shook up, but otherwise okay." His mouth turned grim. "Edna Clauson took the insurance money from her store and moved to Chambersburg with her daughter. Justin and Rorrie are opening their coffee place again, but on the other side of town. Garfield...." He paused and cleared his throat. "Fuck, this is hard. Garfield passed this morning. Something about throwing a clot." Wolf shook his head and inhaled sharply through his nose. "This shit has to stop."

Camshaft agreed. If Crossman and Ratchet hadn't been "on patrol" last night, Bri would probably be dead. This morning, her bookstore was a blackened hull among the other businesses. The spa might also have burned to the ground and quite possibly taken Sabrina with it.

His fists tightened to the point of cramping. The thought of any harm coming to the woman currently sleeping at his house made him want to pound his fists into something until it broke or at least got really bloody.

Wolf let out his breath and laid the gavel on the table. "I got the bylaw template Stud sent me from the Dragon Runners MC. Pretty standard stuff, but we can get to that part later. Specs, we need an update on the rally. The money we raise is gonna make a big difference to the Hob family. Garfield didn't make peanuts, but he wasn't rich either. Mira needs all the help she can get."

Specs grinned widely and stood to give his report. Cam's thoughts were distracted when Ratchet whispered, "Boy Scout," to Crossman. He didn't care. Specs did the best he could to fit in, and right now, his nerdy ADHD was needed.

"I got the permits all squared away. That local band, Spindle 45, is gonna play from noon to three. I tried to get them to play longer, but they have a gig that night. Who knew it took so long to set up microphones and amps and stuff? Anyway, we got four food trucks that will donate all the money they make to the family, less costs. I think that means they'll just give the profits, but that's okay."

Cam tuned out the rambling man. Whatever role he had to play in this rally, he'd play, but at that moment, his focus centered on the woman in his bed. Last night, or rather early this morning, he and Quillon managed—with a lot of cursing and careful movements—to get her van and trailer out of the alley and to his place. Street parking was easiest at that time, and he'd found a spot reasonably close to his house. Later today, he'd move them both in the back near his garage. His spare bedrooms weren't ready for guests, so he'd insisted Sabrina take his bed and he'd sleep on the sofa. Of course, she had to argue with him.

"I ain't takin' your bed, Cam."

"It's not a big deal."

"Yes, it is, sugar. I'll just sleep in my van."

They had a stare-down for several minutes before he spoke again.

"Look, Sabrina, if you're out there by yourself with nothing but a couple lizards for protection, I'm gonna go crazy."

She cocked her head to the side. "Are you doin' that reverse psychology shit on me?"

"Probably, but I'm not kidding. I can't stand the thought of you sleeping in your van when I have a house with an available bed waiting."

Her stance grew rigid as she crossed her arms and dug in. "So I'm supposed to get in your bed for your convenience?"

"That's not what I meant and you know it."

The standoff didn't last long. Exhaustion finally kicked in, and she relented.

"I repeat, I ain't takin' your bed, but I'll compromise. You need to protect me, you can stay with me in the van like we did before."

It was the best he was going to get. "You got it."

This morning, he woke up to a warm female body curled into his side with one arm wrapped over his chest and one leg draped over his thigh. A sense of contentment had welled up in his chest. He could get used to this. The goal now was to get her comfortable in his house so they could be in a real bed and not this small mattress setup.

He'd eased himself out from under her and got

ready for this morning's church meeting. She'd mumbled something before passing back out. He penned a quick note to tell her where he was and ask her to text him when she got up. Before he left, he couldn't resist bending over and brushing his lips on her forehead. It just felt right.

"...Kiss the Knights booth will be on the corner."

Specs's words startled Cam back into the present. "What did you say?"

Quillon suppressed a grin. "Specs decided the young single Knights are gonna man a kissing booth to help raise money. That's Ratchet, Crossman, Stalemate, and you."

"You're kidding, right?"

"Nope." Quillon popped the *p*. "Tickets are five bucks apiece. Better bring your Chapstick. I expect the proceeds will pay off the first *and* second mortgages on Hob's house."

"I'm not doing that."

"Me neither," Crossman agreed.

"But we need at least four to man the booth!" Specs whined.

"Then you do it," Cam growled. "I'm not kissing a bunch of strange women."

Ratchet blinked. "Why not?"

Specs let out what could only be described as a

giggle. "No one wants to kiss me. That's why I chose the good-looking men of the club. The rest are either married or too old."

Melter didn't like that. "Who the fuck are you calling old?"

"All right, pipe down." Wolf banged the gavel with a loud crack. "Let's get back to this. If the only men in the kissing booth are Ratchet and Stalemate, let's nix it and find something else for the club. How 'bout a group ride? Damn, I wish Go-Kart were here. We could use his LED custom work."

Quillon tapped his fingers on the table. "Why don't you call the Dragon Runners and see if that guy Dodge is available? He's the one who does that cool custom painting."

Wolf raised his brows and pursed his lips in a not-a-bad-idea expression. "Pretty short notice, but I'll try. What else we got?"

Cam's phone buzzed in his pocket. He caught Wolf's eye and pointed to the device, then jerked his head to the building's exit. Wolf flicked a finger at the door, indicating he could leave.

Cam fully expected the call to be from Sabrina, but an unfamiliar number popped up. No scam alert, so he answered it.

"Hello?"

At first, the caller stayed silent, but then a raspy voice spoke.

"Hey, baby. S'been a while."

Cam closed his eyes as fear and dread flooded his system. No matter how many times he told her to stop calling him, she always came back eventually. He'd given up hope a long time ago that anything would change, and now this woman no longer had any part in his life, but every so often, she cropped up like a canker sore. Last time she showed up, he had to call the police and have her removed from his front yard. Obviously, she didn't get the message then. He prayed she would stay away from his house this time around.

"Hello, Tammie."

16

Sabrina took a huge cleansing breath of the crisp morning air and let it out slowly. The house she faced differed greatly from Cam's. It looked like the others in this cluttered row: regimented boxes on a thin strip of land with little to no space between them and their neighbors. This one had the luxury of a narrow drive leading to whatever space sat behind it. The place gave off an air of forgotten neglect. No yard to mow, no plants or anything to make the sparse structure appealing in the least. Her bike had a flat tire this morning, so she'd Ubered to this address. One look at the place and she was ready to go back to her van.

This was where Scrap lived—if it could be called that.

More like this is where Scrap exists.

She inhaled again and marched up to the front door. Peeling gray paint flaked off as she knocked on the wood. The man had gone MIA since his episode at the hospital, and she wasn't going to make any more futile efforts to corner him at the bar. After Scrap's collapse, she'd left him alone for a time. Even though she wanted answers, she wouldn't kick a man when he was down.

Whatever happens, I'm gonna keep my dignity and my integrity, she thought as a gruff "Yeah" came from the house's interior. One more big breath and she opened the door.

The inside wasn't much better than the outside. The first floor was an open living area with the kitchen in the back. Beyond that was a bathroom. Narrow stairs led to the upper floor, but by the looks of things, Scrap didn't go up there much.

He was lying back in a beat-up recliner with several afghans tucked around him. The sallow skin on his face wrinkled as he frowned at her. "What the fuck are *you* doing here?"

Sabrina raised her chin and squared her shoulders, as Ernie taught her to do when she faced an opponent. She looked down at the old man in front of her and had a hard time feeling anything but pity for him.

"I came to get answers. I'm not running away from this, and neither are you." She broke the stare to take the few steps over the scratched hardwood floor and plop herself onto the ugly plaid sofa. She had to move a pile of mismatched throw pillows and crumpled bedsheets. "When did you get this thing? When Jesus was a child?"

"Get the fuck out of my house."

"Not until you agree to take the DNA test. I can get one of those mail-order ones from Amazon and have it delivered."

"That's not gonna happen."

"We'll see about that."

Sabrina glanced around at the ancient furnishings. A floor lamp with a shade yellowed with age, a braided rug with colors so faded they'd gone gray, a set of bookshelves stuffed with stacks of old magazines and a few hardbacks. The only modern piece was the flat-screen Vizio mounted above the bricked-over fireplace. Otherwise, the whole house looked like time stopped circa 1975. "Nice place you have here."

Scrap just grunted as he picked up the remote and clicked on the TV. He scrolled through several channels in rapid succession, pausing to view one for a few seconds before moving on to the next. The effect was dizzying. He finally landed on a network that broadcast old game show reruns. Long-dead people competed for prizes already used, broken, and consigned to landfills.

She figured he was trying to intimidate her or annoy her so much that she left. Too bad for him, she had the day off. She crossed her arms and settled herself in for the long haul. "You got any coffee?"

Scrap grunted again.

Sabrina got off the sofa and wandered into the kitchen area. Avocado-green appliances sat next to gold-flake Formica counters, and a chrome-legged kitchen table with the most uncomfortable-looking chairs ever made stood on the opposite side. "Seriously, have you ever thought about joining the twenty-first century and modernizing?"

He jabbed a finger at the entrance. "You don't like my house? There's the fucking door!"

She made her own grunting sound and started rummaging through the cabinets. A cheap four-cup coffee maker sat back against the tiled backsplash. She pulled it forward and dumped the old grounds into a plastic-lined trash can.

"Don't get shit all over my counters!"

The yell almost made her smile.

She found the coffee and the filters in a cabinet, along with several mugs. "You want me to go? There's one guaranteed way."

"I'm not taking a gawddamn test!"

That roar definitely had the corners of her mouth turning up.

"Suit yourself. I kinda like it here in Pittsburgh. I think I'll stick around for a while."

She didn't hear his grumbling reply, but amusement still danced through her head. The new battle plan she'd come up with included letting the man fuss and bluster while she hung around and did the passive-aggressive thing. Whenever she went toe-to-toe with him, he locked down tight. So far, when she didn't pay attention to him, his blowups petered out pretty quickly. This way, she could wear him down until he gave up and gave in.

The coffee maker spit out its goodness, and she sniffed the aroma. Whatever faults Scrap had, bad coffee wasn't one of them.

"Pour me a cup of that."

Sabrina smiled at the gruff demand. She pulled two mugs down from the cabinet and checked them for dust. This machine didn't have an automatic stop, so she deftly transferred one mug under the streaming liquid while filling the other from the pot, then switched them.

"Cream and sugar?"

"Do I look like a cream and sugar kind of man?"

She handed him a full mug. He grunted his thanks while Bob Barker wowed his audience with a new car. The coffee finished bubbling, and she filled her own mug. "I prefer cream and sugar, but I like it black too."

"I don't give a shit."

"Ernie drank his coffee black."

"I don't give a shit about that either."

"Fine. I'm still not leaving."

Scrap opened his mouth to yell at her, but three sharp raps on the front door stopped him.

"Yoo-hoo! Walter, are you decent?" A short, rotund woman somewhere in her seventies bustled in with several brown-paper bags of groceries and a ginormous purse on her arm. When she spotted Sabrina, she stopped and her mouth formed a perfect O.

"Oh, for Pete's sake, I bet you're Raquel's daughter. The one Titus keeps telling me about."

Sabrina smiled as Scrap cursed under his breath. "Yes, I am."

The woman grinned broadly. "So good to finally

meet you. I heard you've made quite the splash. I'm Mary, Titus's wife. You'll know him as Baghouse in their little club." She started putting away the groceries while keeping up a steady stream of conversation. "You look so much like your mother, but I can see Walter there too. You have his eyes and his build. Your mother wasn't curvy at all. No breasts until Walter got her the boob job she wanted. Land sakes, that was a time. Walter took care of her every day until she healed."

"I never knew she had that done."

Mary took out a carton of eggs and put them in the fridge. "It was a long time ago, before you were born. How's your mother doing these days?"

"I don't know. I hardly ever see her." *Confession time,* Sabrina thought as she noticed Scrap was quietly sipping his coffee and listening. That was odd, as she expected him to rage at both her and Mary, but he was keeping to himself, at least for now. "She birthed me and took off. She wasn't around much while I was growing up, just popped in whenever she saw fit."

"I'm sorry to hear that. We were club wives at the same time, but we didn't have much to do with the club or each other, so's I can't tell you much about her from back in the day."

"It's okay." Sabrina lifted her own cup while the woman continued to chatter.

"We got six kids, Titus and me. All boys. Two of 'em are close by, and three others are scattered around the country. One is in the cemetery over in Washington."

Sabrina didn't have to see the woman to hear the sorrow in her voice. "Um... my condolences."

"It happened a few years ago. He was shot while makin' a delivery. Worked for UPS, you see. He wasn't doing anything special, ya know? No cause for the greater good. Just dropping off a big box of T-shirts and got caught in some gang war thing. Shot in the neck. Here one day and gone the next." Mary kept bustling around the kitchen, putting boxes in cupboards and wiping the counter.

Sabrina had no clue what to say to that. "I'm really sorry for your loss."

Mary wiped a finger under one eye and dipped her head. "I appreciate you saying that. I really do. I still miss him, but he left behind a piece of himself with our daughter-in-law and our cute little grandson. Portia and Grayson are such a comfort to us. I don't know what we'd do without family around, especially when times get tough."

Sabrina had the notion that Mary's conversation

just dropped a lot of hints, but she wasn't sure if the message was actually meant for her.

Scrap evidently thought the same thing. "Woman, if you're trying to fucking say something, just spit it out and be done with it."

Mary jerked open a cabinet door, making it smack loudly into its neighbor and causing Sabrina to jump. "You haven't moved from that chair since I got here and I bet not since she got here either. Wanna tell us why?"

"Do not fucking go there."

The words were supposed to be a threat, but Sabrina heard a note of desperation in his growling tone.

Mary ignored it. She shoved several canned goods into the cabinet and slammed it shut. "I lost my son years ago, and I feel that pain every damn day. You have a living, breathing daughter right here, and you're wasting time you don't have."

"I'm warning you, Mary. Shut the fuck up."

But Mary didn't heed the barked order. "You want me to shut up? How 'bout you come over here and shut me up? You can't, can you?"

"Ma-reeee!"

The woman ignored the drawn-out growl.

"Because you're afraid you pissed yourself again. Am I right?"

"Gawddammit, Mary!"

Sabrina's brain took a minute to process. "What? Why? What's going on?"

Mary's mouth pressed into a grim line. "He's had diabetes for decades and never paid attention or took care of himself very well. Now he's got kidney disease and is too bullheaded to tell anyone."

"That's my fucking business!" Scrap snarled.

But Mary did not back down. "It's not just your business. It's my business. It's Titus's business. It's the club's business." She pointed at Sabrina. "Most of all, it's *her* business. She needs something from you that will bring her peace. I do not understand how you, of all people, can't see that."

Scrap spluttered. "How do you know all this shit?"

"I've been married to Titus for fifty-three years. Yinz know we talk to each other. He's really worried about you and the club. Mostly about you." She moved to stand over Scrap and put her hands on her generous hips. "You are so alone, Walter. You rattle around this house or that damn bar like a zombie just waiting to die. Now you have a chance to regain some family, and you're pissing it away. Take the damn DNA test and confirm what we already know."

"No!"

"Why not?"

"I fucking said no!"

"And I fucking asked why not?"

Scrap lost it. "Because, if I *am* her father, that means I abandoned *my only gawddamn child*!"

Silence grew thick after the older man's roar. Sabrina's ears rang, and once again she found herself processing new information. "I never learned about you until my dad, Ernie, passed away. Did… um… did you know about me?"

Scrap seemed to shrink and age. In a matter of seconds, his face morphed from a raging beet red to a remorseful pale white. "Raquel sent me pictures every time she called to ask for money. I gave her some 'cause I thought there was a chance. Then I found out she did the same thing to three other men. Claimed you were theirs and wanted child support. She was playing a fucking game with all of us, including Ernie. So I stopped playing and told her to fuck off."

Sabrina swallowed. "She fucked with both of us, then. She left not too long after I was born. Ernie got full custody of me before I turned one. To my knowledge, she never paid him a dime. If she collected child support from anyone, it was a money thing for herself." She held up both hands and spread her fingers. "I can count on my hands the times I've seen her during my life. She's a shit parent 'cause she chose to be one. I'm thinking now that same choice was made *for* you, not *by* you. Am I close?"

Scrap breathed hard and deep, the air sawing out of his nose in long wheezes. His lips were twitching, as if he was trying to hold himself back. Mary openly cried and pulled a tissue from her pocket.

Sabrina fought her throat closing up. She didn't want to cry. Not yet, and not in front of this man. "I don't blame you for not believing Raquel. I'm not surprised at all by what she did to you and others. I'm still gonna say I... no, *we* need to find out the truth. I think I deserve it. I think you do too."

There ya go, Scrap. I lobbed the ball in your court. It's up to you if you want to be a shit father or not.

He swallowed and coughed several times, sniffing and clearing. Sabrina noticed when he raised a hand to brush away some moisture that had gathered under his eyes. He muttered something in his rumbling voice.

Mary leaned forward. "What did you say?"

"I said I'd take the fucking test."

Sabrina left Scrap's house, but instead of going back to Cam's place, she decided to walk for a bit. Thoughts and scenarios filled her head with possibilities, and it was giving her a major headache. A dull pain pulsed behind her eyes as she meandered through the narrow streets.

He's gonna take the test.
What if I'm not his daughter after all?
What if I am?
Is he dying?

Her phone rang. The area code was from Florida, and she answered the unknown number, thinking it might be important.

Instead, she got an earful of Spanish cussing.

"*Qué te pasa? Estupida!*" ("What's wrong with you? Stupid!")

"Well, hello to you, too, Rosa." Anger flashed through Sabrina's body with enough force that she started to sweat. The last person she wanted to deal with on this fucked-up day was her estranged aunt.

"Rodrigo has papers for you to sign."

"Congratulations."

"This is no joke. They must be signed soon."

Sabrina stood on the sidewalk and looked

around, seeing how far she'd gone in the unfamiliar neighborhood. "Y'all need me to sign something? I'll tell you the same thing I told Rodrigo: Bring them to me or mail them."

"No, you must come here and sign them. Immediately!"

With the stress from keeping her job, her current living arrangement, an unfamiliar state, a big question mark on her personal life with Cam, and the discovery of Scrap's failing health, Sabrina had reached her emotional limit. She opened her mouth and let loose. "You know what, *Tia*? I have no fucks left to give about you or Rodrigo or the whole fucking family. I'm in fucking Pennsylvania, trying to find a new life and get the truth from a man who's got kidney disease and might be dying. I don't have money or time to come to Florida. Y'all wanted me out, remember? I'm fucking out. If you want my signature on anything at all, you or Rodrigo needs to bring your happy asses up here. Otherwise, I'm. Fucking. Done!"

She hung up and blocked the number. Only then did she start to shake.

She brought her arms up to hug herself as she observed her surroundings. Old run-down row houses that hadn't seen any updates or even a coat of paint stood on either side of the rough, broken street. This was the type of place where cops seldom came. There were very few people out and about this late afternoon, but those who were eyed her with either suspicion or speculation. She turned to go back the way she came and find Scrap's house again but got twisted up even further.

Shit, I do not need to be here. Angry tears formed in her eyes, but she refused to let them fall.

There's a map on your phone, dummy. Use it to figure out where you are and how to get back to where you need to be.

Of course, her phone showed the red line of death. Three percent power left on 5G meant shutdown was imminent. Thinking quickly, she dialed Cam.

"What's up?"

At his voice, her throat closed and whatever bravado she had vanished. "I don't know where I am." That was all she could say.

"Shit. Can you see a street sign?"

She squinted at the corner. "Lowrie is the only name I can see."

"Can you stay where you are? It's gonna take me about twenty minutes to get there and find you."

"I... I don't know. My phone is almost dead."

"There's a cemetery on that road. Find it and wait there. No one should bother you if you're sitting at someone's grave."

"Okay."

"Sabrina, hang in there. I'm on my way."

She hung up just before the screen went dead.

"I'm on my way."

His words acted like a balm to her nerves. She found the cemetery. It was small and not particularly maintained, but there was a bench facing the old headstones. She sat and did some relaxing breaths, concentrating on releasing the tension from her body.

Scrap has diabetes and kidney disease. What does that mean for me? Should I feel sorry for him? Should I not care at all?

The elaborate gravestone in front of her had no answers.

Scrap's attitude toward her sucked, but she vividly remembered his words. The tone and the volatile emotion behind them.

"If I am her father, *that means I* abandoned *my only gawddamn child!"*

Ernie had been her anchor and the only person who ever truly cared for her. Scrap was a mean, cantankerous asshole, but perhaps, just perhaps, there might be a tiny bit of redeeming quality somewhere. It was probably a futile hope, but at this point, she'd take anything she could get.

The cloudy sky darkened more, and the wind picked up a bit. The squirrely weather mentioned possible showers tonight. Hopefully, Cam would get her soon. Was there more than one cemetery on this street?

Her thoughts wandered to Cam. He would be happy that Scrap agreed to the test at last, but what about the other stuff? Should she tell him?

A few raindrops splattered onto the rough granite in front of her. *Great. Just fucking great.* She sighed and placed a hand over her eyes to peer at the sky. *Can you please hold off just a little while longer?*

The answer came back as bigger, more frequent drops. The only missing part to make her day worse would be a call from Rodrigo once her phone was charged.

She did wonder about her aunt's insistence to sign whatever papers Rodrigo had. What exactly were they trying to pull, and why was her signature so important?

A familiar rumble came to her ears, and she spotted Cam coming slowly down the street. He stopped in front of the gated area and dismounted in one fluid motion. "Are you okay?"

"It seems like you're always coming to my rescue."

"And I always will."

He folded her in his arms, and his mouth came down to hers. The kiss wasn't sexual, more of a confirmation. It said "I'm here" in a way that bore an intimacy outweighing sex. He tasted strongly of mint, and she guessed he had a box of Altoids in his pocket.

The skies opened up and rain poured over them, but neither made a move to run. Even in a storm, he had her back. She felt solid, whole in this connection. If there was ever any question or doubt, it was gone. Cam belonged to her and she to him. The realization was thrilling, terrifying, and satisfying all at the same time.

"Sorry it took me so long," he murmured into her ear. "I grabbed your helmet before I came."

"You're here now, and that's all that matters," she breathed. The cold rain continued to douse them both, but warmth filled her inside. No, that was heat. Real heat. "Take me home."

17

Rain pelted them on the way to the house, but the full-face helmets kept them pain-free from the stinging bullets. Sabrina's hair was a tangled mess as she didn't bother to braid it, just stuffed the wet mass into the padding before they took off from the cemetery.

They only made it as far as the front door before she made the first move, jumping into Cam's arms and kissing him long and hard. A trail of water and sopping-wet clothes tracked through the house, marking their journey to his bedroom, starting with shoes and socks dropped at the door.

Cam jerked his shirt over his head and left it at the bottom of the staircase. The phone call with Tammie disappeared from his mind as his focus centered completely on Sabrina. Her body, her needs, and her demands. She pulled her own shirt over her head, taking the sports bra with it. Her freed breasts teased him with their tight mauve nipples, and his dick flared to life.

"We need to slow down, babe."

She turned and sprinted up the steps, shucking off her jeans and throwing them over the railing as she moved. "I want this, sugar. Have no doubt about it." His eyes zeroed in on her bouncing ass as she ran.

Piece after piece of clothing dropped, so by the time they hit the bed, they were both naked and on each other in a frenzy.

Cam kissed her wildly with a hunger that she matched move for move. His fantasies about how their first time would go blew up in his face. He thought he would be cooking for her, slowly teasing her with a long night of seduction before taking her to bed, and only then sealing the deal after playing with her body and drawing out the pleasure as long as possible.

He quickly discovered she had other plans. She pulled him down, spreading her legs and opening her bare pussy to him. Her hands were everywhere on his body as he hovered over her, supporting himself on his elbows while he tried to slow down.

"Let me get you ready, baby," he panted as she clutched at his back to pull him close.

"I am ready," she breathed in a husky, needy voice. She wrapped her thighs around his hips and gyrated her core against him as proof.

His dick hung heavy between his legs and brushed against her wetness. "I want to take you slow. Make it good."

"Do slow later. I need you now." She followed her order by tightening the grip of her legs around him.

Her heat burned against his hard flesh. "You want this, you got it." He pulled himself slightly up, losing contact for a moment.

She made a thin sound as she watched him reach for his nightstand. "What are you doing?"

"Condom." His voice was gruff as he tore open the plastic square with his teeth and worked his hand between them. "Let me loose for a minute." He rolled it on with one hand in the fraction of space she allowed him.

"Cam, I don't want to wait any longer. Take me now!" Her demand couldn't be any clearer.

He lined himself up and pushed inside her

soaked channel. She let out a long, high-pitched moan and clutched at his waist to pull him farther into her. She was tight, wet, and warm, and it was all he could do to keep from coming in three seconds.

Sabrina, of course, showed no compunction to restrain herself. She writhed against him, lifting and grinding her hips until, with a keening cry, she came. Feeling her pulse around him was more than he could take, and his own voice joined hers a few moments later.

It was faster than he'd ever climaxed in his life.

It was harder than he'd ever come before.

It was a deeper satisfaction than he'd ever experienced.

He hoped with every molecule of his soul that she felt the same. If not, he would do his absolute best to make damn sure she did. "Christ, I'm sorry, baby. Too fast. I wanted to—"

She cut him off with a kiss. "That was perfect." She reached as far down his back and buttocks as she could and grabbed a double handful. "You're perfect. There's so much I want to do with you. To you. Not just tonight. Wanna try?"

He'd just come, but his dick was already planning round two. The box of condoms was old, and he forgot how many were in it, but he hoped there were enough left.

"Absolutely, but we're doing it my way this time."

Sabrina snuggled under Cam's arm into his warm side. She was sore as hell, but the good kind of sore. After the explosive first round, he showed her exactly what he meant by slow. Her nipples were still rosy red from his mouth and hands. When she tried to get him to hurry, he held her hands over her head and kept licking and sucking until she was begging for him to take her again.

"Not yet, baby."

He'd gone down to spread the folds between her legs and work magic. He teased and held her teetering on the edge of coming over and over.

"Not yet, baby."

His fingers slid through her wetness inside her, delving and exploring.

"Not yet, baby."

He pulled those digits out, coated with her juices, and reached farther back, touching a part of her no man had ever touched before. Pressing, asking for entrance.

"Not yet, baby."

There was a slight burning as he breached her there. One that ignited all her senses and centered her focus on one thing only: him.

"Now."

Twice more he made her come, once with his mouth and then with his body. One climax was so intense she actually bit him on the shoulder. Had she ever let anyone have this much control over her? Allowed this level of intimacy? Yes, she'd had encounters in the past, but not on this level. Whatever bond she'd developed with him had gained strength in the short time she'd known him. Her trust was practically nonexistent with people in general, but with Cam, there were no limits and no taboos. Mind-blowing possibilities existed that she'd never thought would be a part of her life. It was scary as hell, but at the same time, she couldn't wait for whatever came next.

She stirred against him, and his arm squeezed around her. "You doin' okay, sweetheart?"

She nuzzled into his neck and paused to examine the teeth marks she'd left. "Damn, I'm sorry, sugar."

He chuckled. "I'm not. I'm thinking that's my new

goal: to make you come so hard, you'll bite me every time."

A predatory smile curled up on her lips. "Maybe I'll pull a reverse and make *you* come that hard."

"Challenge accepted." He jackknifed up, and she got a prime view of his back tattoo. "You hungry?"

"Are you cooking?"

He grinned. "Yeah, I got stuff I can make in the fridge."

"Then I'm hungry."

He slipped on a pair of old gray sweatpants but left his shirt off. "I'll go down and get started. Feel free to explore."

"Mind if I grab one of your T-shirts?"

"Help yourself."

She snagged one with a faded Steelers logo on it and followed him downstairs to the main floor.

Sabrina liked his house. This suburb was nice and clean, and on the outskirts of where Attic and all the messy stuff took place. Just like its neighbors, the house was tall and long and sat on a hill. Steps were required to enter the main floor from the front or the back where they usually came in, with a kitchen that opened into a large living space. The second level was a loft that had two smaller bedrooms on either side that were currently filled with boxes of stuff and other junk that every household had but never got rid of. The master was the best part—a third-level converted attic that ran the entire length of the house and sported a bay window that had a nice view of the river in the distance.

As they descended the iron spiral staircase, they picked up the clothing items they'd discarded on the way up.

"You want to dump these in the dryer or start a wash load?" He pointed with a fistful of her bra and panties. "There's a basket in there already that's pretty full."

"Washing sounds better."

She carried the wet clothing to the mudroom and dumped it into the machine. Her face broke into a smile when she spotted the basket was a mix of both of their items. She glanced out the back-door window where a two-bay detached garage sat. The yard was big and enclosed by a tall privacy fence. Her van was parked on the gravel-filled pad next to the garage.

Sabrina's eyes darted to the space between the house and the vehicle. "Think I can dash over to my place and grab some more of my clothes?"

"I'll get them for you after we eat, yeah?"

He'd pulled a couple of chicken breasts in a

brown spicy marinade along with several bags of salad vegetables from the fridge and piled them on the dark gray granite counter.

"Did you do all the renovations here yourself? Did you pick out the furniture?" she asked, seating herself across from him as he worked.

He poured two cups of water into a pot, set it on a burner, and clicked on the gas. "Yeah. Did the floors too. And the painting."

The shine from the pretty gray-and-tan grain blended with the pale gray-blue of the walls. One color throughout the main floor and loft. The spare bedrooms were different, one green and one a pale rose. "That's impressive. I'm surprised a rental would let you do that."

"I own it."

"Really? Why didn't I know this already?"

He dumped a cup of rice into the heating water and stirred it. "Yup. My foster parents left it to us boys, and I bought out the others to keep it. Kyle and Morgan are older than me and moved out years before I did. They have their own places and lives. Tammie—" He hesitated, like he needed to force himself to say the words. "Tammie wasn't interested."

He pulled out a cutting board and placed a head

of broccoli on it. The knife in his hand had a gray-and-black blade of layered metals in a pretty criss-cross pattern. The striking sheen contrasted with the pale wood handle. It fit Cam's hand as if it was made for him. Hell, it probably was.

"Is that one of your blades?" she asked, snagging a green floret.

He smiled and tossed one into his mouth as well. "Yeah, I made this one. One of my first attempts at a Damascus wave." He set the prepped broccoli in a cooking dish and cut up more veggies with the pretty knife. The sharp edge slid through a green pepper like it was butter. He held the blade up to the light to show its intricacies better. "Turned out nice, and I decided to keep this one for myself. I think it's a lot like me."

"What do you mean?"

"To get this effect, I had to cut thin layers of high-carbon and low-carbon steel. I also added some nickel alloys for a better contrast. Built them up and forged them together. Slow heat, borax flux, and a lot of hammering once the metal got to temperature. Then I had to cut it, fold it in half, and start the process again and again until I made a couple hundred or so layers. It takes a lot of time to form a usable billet."

He finished with the green pepper and started on a red one. "I think our lives are built on layers like this. We have our high times, and we have our low times. Eventually, it all comes together to create who we are."

She picked up one of the pepper slices and crunched it between her front teeth. The crisp flavor filled her mouth. "Interesting analogy."

He smiled and sprayed a large skillet with oil. "There's a lot more to it. Forming a blade means heating and hammering, reheating and more hammering, but"—he held up a pointer finger—"you have to be careful. Too much heat or hammering and the blade might shatter. Not enough heat on the initial billet and the layers can come apart. It's tricky and takes patience. I don't think people have that anymore."

Sabrina let out a short hum. "I can agree with that."

The chicken sizzled as he added it to the pan. He lowered the temperature on the rice and put a lid on the pot. "Finishing involves grinding away all the parts that aren't needed and sharpening the edge to uniform perfection. Again, this takes time and attention to detail."

The cooking meat had a spicy aroma. He put the

chopped broccoli in the microwave to steam while he took out a head of lettuce from the fridge. "The blade has to be hardened. That means one more round of heating to temperature and oil-quenching to make it flexible, but solid and unbreakable."

He raised the lettuce high in the air and slammed the bottom onto the counter. Sabrina jumped at the sudden movement and stared when he turned over the green head and easily pulled out the core. "That's pretty nifty."

"Work smarter, not harder, right?" He picked up the knife again and sliced the head in half. "I learned that bit from my foster mom. She's the one who taught us how to cook."

"You mentioned Kyle, Morgan, and Tammie."

He nodded and expertly diced the lettuce. "Cecil and Vera couldn't have kids, so they chose to raise other people's children. We were the last ones they took on because of their age. Vera became my mom, and Cecil became my dad. I was nine years old when I met Vera. She brought me cookies and explained her rules and what she would do for me. I left the children's home at four forty in the afternoon and went home with her."

Sabrina made the connection immediately. "The time on your tattoo."

One corner of Cam's mouth shifted up. "Yeah. I didn't know it then, but that's when my life started. Cecil and Vera treated me like a person. I had a place and a routine and people who loved and supported me." He nodded at the dining alcove. "There used to be a big table over there. We did homework there every night. All of us. They both sat with us to help. Dinner. Board games. Family talks." He smiled. "Yeah, they called us family. I have a lot of good memories from that table. That was the one piece of furniture Morgan wanted. Since I got the house, I figured it was fair."

Sabrina's heart cracked at the poignant words coming from the man who grew up here. "I think Ernie did the same for me. I don't know when he started doubting he was my real father, but he never treated me as less than his daughter. Kids need assurance, right?"

Cam nodded as he stirred the cooked rice and dumped it into a bowl. "I guess that's why I like working with metal so much. If you forge steel the right way, it holds its edge and stays stable for a lifetime."

He clicked off the burners and raised his eyes to hers. Sabrina's breath caught at what reflected in them.

"I really want to see what we're going to forge together. We've come to that point where there's no going back and you'll stay here with me."

"I understand."

"Are you sure? You'll *stay here* with me."

Sabrina got it completely. Cam would become her man, her anchor, her family—permanently. She would put down roots in this community and make a home she wouldn't have to leave.

"I'm ready."

18

This time of year could be tricky with snow, sleet, or sunshine, but fortune smiled upon the Knights. The day of the rally dawned with a nice cloudless day with slightly warmer temperatures than were usual for this time of year. Perfect for the event.

"Pretty fucking amazing, yeah?" Crossman remarked as they waited in line for coffee at the Dapper Bean coffee truck. Several more trucks had set up in spots around the neighborhood park. Pizza, tacos, corn dogs, and funnel cakes were available. Kids had a face-painting booth and a long row of carnival type games. Several local crafters were scattered around selling doodads like soap, candles, and jewelry.

"Specs outdid himself," Cam agreed.

The turnout surprised him, but it pleased him too. The club's display included some vintage and custom bikes and the opportunity to take pictures while sitting on them. Cash already filled the donation jar next to the Harley Fatboy, and the clock hadn't hit noon yet.

Kiss the Knights had turned into a Date Knight raffle. Ratchet, Crossman, Melter, and Stalemate agreed to take four winners on some sort of date that involved a ride on the back of their motorcycle—after his night with Sabrina, Cam had pulled his name from the single-bikers category. Crossman mentioned going through Wheeling, West Virginia. Roughly an hour out, some sort of food, and an hour back. The outings were supposed to be scheduled for the next weekend as long as the weather held out. Cam didn't consider a date with a Knight to be a big deal, but apparently it was, seeing as the paper tickets were almost sold out.

Two screaming kids ran past them with balloon animals in their hands, their dad chasing after them. Cam watched them go and wondered what Scrap was up to. He hadn't been around the club since his hospital stay. Sabrina had gone by his house to confront him, but she hadn't told him anything about what happened. This relationship was too new, and Cam had no intention of rocking any boats. He had baggage himself he needed to share with her when they got to the full-disclosure phase. He wanted to give her the same respect, but he had so many questions about her meeting with Scrap and how she'd ended up in that emotional state when he found her.

She did tell him she'd met Mary, Baghouse's wife. That was news to him, as he didn't know Baghouse was married.

Cam frowned as the line moved forward. Communication needed to improve within the club. Baghouse feeling the need to keep that part of his life a secret was weird. The extent of Melter's drug habits also bugged him. Scrap's absence made Cam think something serious was going on. He got the part about being private, but if anything concerned the club, he and the rest of the Knights needed to know about it.

Specs bustled by with a clipboard in his hands and a big grin on his bespectacled face. "We're way under budget for this. So cool!"

Cam held back his amusement at the nerdy little

guy. "That's fantastic, Specs. You've done a great job with everything."

The man puffed out his chest and preened. "It's for a good cause, right?"

"Absolutely. Want a coffee?"

Specs shook his head. "Nah, I'm good. Got the adrenaline going, n'at. I'll see yous later."

Cam and Crossman got to the barista, and both were surprised to see Jazz manning the food truck.

"Hiya, guys. I'm helping Rorrie today, so don't look at me like that. It's been cranking all morning, and he needed some extra hands." Jazz's signature blue hair showed dark brown roots, as was expected in the growing-out process.

"I'll get a latte with extra foam and a shot of vanilla," Crossman ordered as he pulled out his wallet.

"On the house, boys. Yinz just keep watching and helping. What's for you, Cam?"

"Do you make plain coffee?"

Jazz blinked. "Well... um... yeah?"

"Then I want two large coffees. One black, one cream and sugar."

She laughed. "Okay, I get it. Coming right up."

Coffees in hand, the two men wandered through

the crowded park. People were walking and talking with big smiles on their faces. The band set up early and had started their first set exactly at noon. A group of kids were dancing with wild abandon to music from the eighties and nineties—songs so old they were popular with their parents and grandparents but were still rocking even today.

Off to one side of the park, between an essential oils seller and a leathersmith, the spa had brought in two massage chairs. A tall and thin African American man rubbed down a large woman whose ample figure spilled over the seat. Sabrina worked on her twin, who appeared even larger.

"Hey, babe, I brought you a coffee. Should still be hot."

Sabrina paused to take a healthy swallow before continuing to press into the woman's shoulders. "How are you doing, Emma?"

The woman giggled. "I'm doing great. Even better now. I bought a whole roll of raffle tickets for the Date Knight thing. I'm sooooo hoping I'll win!"

Cam's first thought was if she did, whoever got her would have to put extra shocks on his bike. "I hope you do too."

Emma giggled again.

"Okay, milady, your time is up," Sabrina said. "I hope you feel better."

The woman rolled her massive shoulders. "Oh, yes! Much better. Do you have a card?"

Sabrina handed her one, and Cam noticed her name was on them. He grinned at the small confirmation that she planned on sticking around. Her presence in his life had formed into a comfortable habit, and he liked it. A lot.

"How's it been today?" he asked once Emma was gone.

Sabrina squirted some sanitizer into her palm from a nearby table full of supplies. "My hands haven't hurt like this in a long time. Stephan and I are doing fifteen minutes for fifteen dollars, and people have been coming at us all day."

She reached one arm forward and used her other hand to bend back her fingers toward her elbow in a long stretch.

Cam waited until she finished shaking out her arms and hands before passing the coffee back to her. "Good business, then?"

Her grin showed pure happiness. "Yes, it's been great. We've booked a lot of new clients today. Cicely will be thrilled." She looked around at the crowd of people. "I don't know a lot about rallies, but this is one of the best block parties I've ever been to. Y'all have outdone yourselves."

Cam smiled at the compliment. Yeah, he was pleased at the turnout and the show of support. It was a shame it had to come from a tragedy. Everyone here loved the hardworking and gentle Garfield, and his death left a hole in many lives, but seeing so many people come together to support his wife and kids meant the world.

Perhaps this was the direction the Knights needed and the basis for their purpose. Wolf spoke often of the tight brotherhood of the Dragon Runners MC and how they thrived in both business and community. From what little Cam had learned about the North Carolina club, they might not always follow the law, but they were always fair. He thought that was a pretty good balance.

Crossman helped the other woman from Stephan's massage chair.

"Thanks for that," she said, then studied him for a beat. "Hey, aren't you one of the Date Knight Knights?"

Crossman's face froze. "Um, yes? Yes, I am."

A huge grin lifted the woman's second chin. "You are soooo cute! I hope I win you!"

"Uh... I hope you do too," Crossman answered awkwardly.

"Never mind that now," Stephan interrupted while wiping down the angled chair and headrest with sanitizer. "It's this man's turn, so let me get my hands on him, yeah?"

The masseuse bustled Crossman into position and started pressing on his shoulders. "I bought some of those date tickets myself. *I* might win you."

Crossman groaned as Stephan dug into his muscles. "I'm not gay, but I'll definitely take you for a ride if you keep that up."

"Oooooh, keep talking, honey."

Cam laughed as he drained the last bit of his coffee before tossing the paper cup into a nearby trash can. He turned back to an amused Sabrina. "Wanna take a break and go see the other stuff?"

"Absolutely. Hey, Stephan? Text me if you get a bunch of people and need me, okay?"

He nodded. "Will do. Now go away."

Cam took Sabrina's hand as they walked, threading his fingers between hers and swinging gently. He bought them loaded hot dogs from a food truck and watched as she took a big bite. Immediately, the mass of toppings splooged out, making a total mess on her pink shirt.

She laughed and swiped off the mustard and relish. "Eat a little, wear the rest," she joked.

He handed her a pile of napkins. "I hope no one sees me in public with you like this."

She scrunched her face at him. "Why? Will I bring down your street cred?"

He choked on the bite he'd just taken. "What the hell is street cred?"

"I don't know. I heard it in a movie once." She looked around for a trash bin to toss the soiled napkins, finding one near an ice cream vendor.

"You're nuts," he said as they headed that way.

"And you love every minute."

Yes, I do.

"Mind if I ask you something?"

She eyed the ice cream menu. "Anything, as long as I get one of those butterscotch dipped cones."

"Wanna tell me what happened with Scrap the other day that had you wandering around a strange place in tears?"

Her face fell. "I want to tell you everything, but I don't think it's my place to share Scrap's personal business. I will tell you that he said he'd take the test. Sometime next week."

Cam blinked and then grinned at her as they

waited for their cones. "That sounds great. What made him change his mind?"

She hesitated. "I'm sorry, Cam. I think if I tell you about what's happening in Scrap's private life, he would get really upset. I don't know all the details, but it's his story to tell the club when he's ready to share. I don't like secrets, but I feel like I have to keep this one, at least for now."

"Does it have an effect on the Knights?"

She sighed as she reached up to take the two ice cream cones from the vendor. "I don't know. Like I said, it's his story to tell."

Cam furrowed his brow, but he understood where she was coming from. He wouldn't want his personal business run through the gossip mill any more than it already was. "All right, I'll stop pushing. What else is bothering you?"

She handed him one of the cones and lifted the other to her mouth to take a big bite of the hardened candy shell. "Well, my family. Rodrigo is still bugging me about Dad's estate. Says I have to sign something, and he wants me to come home to do it. Aunt Rosa called me too. For people who wanted me out of the family, they really can't seem to leave me alone."

They started a slow walk away from the vendor

and back to the massage booth area. Cam's eyes followed her tongue as she licked around the base of the cone. A short fantasy movie rolled through his mind, and he indulged himself for a few moments, then had to replay her words before responding. He snagged a handful of napkins to cover his lapse of focus. "Want me to come with you?"

"I'm not planning any road trips. I told you I'm on the outs with them, remember? If he needs my signature, then he can come get it. It's just another annoyance since he's been texting and calling me about it. And now my aunt too."

"If you change your mind, let me know."

"I appreciate that." She paused and broke off another piece of butterscotch, slurping at the melted ice cream. "The rest is me. I don't know what I'm doing or where I'm going. I'm not thrilled with working at Cicely's place, but I'm getting a lot of really good clients who like my services. That's a big thing in my world. And then there's you."

She stopped walking and turned to face him directly. "I'm not gonna play games or bullshit you. I like you. A lot. I like being at your house. I like talking with you. I like how you support and help me with no questions or hidden motives. Sometimes, when I think about that, I get a little overwhelmed that anyone would do that for me."

Cam took a big bite of his cone and crunched through the rest of the shell. "Isn't it obvious yet, babe? I like you, too, and I want to help you."

Her eyes shifted down to the white rivulets oozing over her fingers. "I'm so messed up right now, Cam. I want to be with you... like *be* with you, but I'm not sure what's gonna happen next week or even tomorrow. I don't want to start something I can't finish or lead you on or set myself up for heartache. But I'm in your space already, and I'm scared I've already done that to myself by sleeping with you."

Cam took one of the flimsy napkins and wiped her sticky fingers. "Do you have any absolute deal-breakers?"

"Like what?"

"Like no dogs or cats?"

"I have my dragons, but I'm not opposed to other pets."

He tossed the used napkins into a trash can. "Any kind of music you hate?"

"Not really."

"Pet peeves?"

She bit into the side of the cone before answering. "I can't stand people chewing with their mouths open. Body odor, like unwashed—ugh, it gives me the willies. Bad manners, and giving service people a hard time just because you can. That pisses me off."

He chuckled. "Anything else?"

She shared his amusement. "I'm sure I have others, but those are the big ones that come to mind."

"Well, I don't chew with my mouth open. I get dirty at work, but I shower every day. I make a point of being polite and respectful to everyone, but I confess that I've enjoyed tossing out the few men who turn asshole on the dancers at the bar."

"Hmmm. And you're telling me this why?"

He raised a hand to cup her cheek, and she let him touch her. Their eyes met, and the seriousness of the moment made the rest of the world disappear. "You wanna know what I think? We should just let life happen and see where we go. If there's a problem, we'll handle it. I don't want to miss out on something good just because I'm too scared to take a chance."

"What if it doesn't work out?"

"What if it does?" He hoped his low voice carried the sincerity she needed to hear. "Take a chance with me, Sabrina."

Her lips parted to give him an answer.

Rat-tat-tat-tat-tat!

Shit! That's gunfire!

Cam's entire body locked as he pulled Sabrina down and into his chest, his eyes darting to find the source. Two more cracks identified the shooter was on the other side of the park. People started screaming and running willy-nilly with no thought or direction.

He held her close and shouted as loud as he could, jabbing and pointing in the opposite direction. "That way! Find cover behind the food trucks! Call 911!"

The chaotic throng listened to him and headed for the row of broad, heavy vehicles.

"You go too." He gave Sabrina a push.

"Come with me!" Her face had drained of blood, and she held on to one of his hands with both of hers.

"There's still people over there, babe."

Another couple of shots sounded. Shouts from the Knights mixed with the fearful cries from the civilians. Cam spotted Wolf and Quillon making their way through the panicked crowd, facing the danger and putting themselves between the shooter and their prey.

"Are you crazy?"

He ignored her question. "Help with crowd control, yeah? Try to calm everyone down."

"Cam?" Her voice wavered. Tears filled her eyes, and he had no more time to debate with her.

He seized the back of her neck and brought his mouth down on hers in a firm kiss. It was brief, but he was making a point. "I'll come back to you, baby. I promise."

He turned and sprinted to catch up to Wolf and Quillon, and they hid behind the dubious cover of a picnic table. Two people were on the ground, still alive but screaming in pain. Another man staggered across the open area, clutching his bleeding arm. A terrified child sat in the giant sandbox, crying hard and looking around.

"Bennie!" a woman yelled. She tried to run to her child, but she had a baby strapped to her front.

Fuck. Cam darted out of his cover to block the woman before she made herself a target.

"I'll get him. You stay here."

A panicked cry came from her lips as several more bullets cracked through the air. Someone shrieked in pain, and Cam spotted Stephan lying behind his massage chair with both hands around his leg.

"The shooter is somewhere on the roof of those

storage buildings. I can't tell which one," Quillon shouted behind him.

Shit. "I'm going for the kid," Cam yelled to his brothers. "Are either of you packing?"

Quillon nodded. "Ever since that shit went down with Tracie, I keep my Luger with me at all times."

"You know I don't do guns anymore. I'll spot for you," Wolf told him while dialing his phone. "Ratchet? The shooter is on one of the storage building rooftops. You can see all three from the pier at the reservoir. See if you can find him." He clicked off. "Ready when you are, Cam."

Cam took three large breaths and then took off running toward the kid. Another crack sounded, and a streak of heat flew by his ear. *Fuck me, that's close!* He grabbed the kid by the arms and hugged him tight as he ran to the tree line with the intent of getting behind one of the oaks. Thankfully, the boy didn't struggle, as wrestling an octopus would have made it much harder.

He was almost at his goal when two more shots rang out, one after the other. This time he felt a burn across his left arm and he stumbled, twisting to land on his back and protect the boy. After he hit the ground, he rolled and put the kid under him. "Stay still," he panted.

"Mommy!"

"She's okay. We'll go get her in a minute, yeah?"

Sirens pierced the air, and in minutes the place was surrounded by cops and paramedics. Policemen ran by, guns drawn. Cam flinched, waiting for one of them to kick him off the boy, but they passed by, heading to the storage buildings.

"Stay put!" an officer barked at him.

No problem. His arm throbbed, and he wiggled around to grab it.

"You're bleeding," the little boy observed.

It surprised Cam how calm the child had become. "I guess I am."

"You hafta put a Band-Aid on it."

"I'll get one as soon as I can."

The boy stared at Cam's hand as it clutched at the wound. "Gotta be a big one."

Calls of "Clear" rang out, and Cam rolled off the kid. He bit his lip at the pain. "I think your mom is over—"

"Bennie!"

Once mother and son were reunited, they were bustled off to see one of the medical people. Quillon helped Cam to his feet to do the same. Cam noticed the man's rigid posture and remembered Quillon went through a similar scene a couple of years ago.

The good part? He met his wife, Tracie. The bad part? People died.

"How bad?"

Cam cursed at the achy sting that zapped him with every step he took. Even though the endorphins had kicked in, it still hurt like a mother. "Fuck! I'm not swinging a hammer anytime soon."

Quillon helped stabilize Cam's injured side as they slowly walked to the medical area. "Wolf took off to find Ratchet and get a status. He said Denny's here and arguing with someone over jurisdiction."

"Like we need that shit right now." Cam couldn't help his bitter tone. He wasn't dying, but he hurt pretty fucking badly. "Can you find Sabrina?"

"I can try. Sit your ass down here. The medics will see you in a minute."

Cam raised his gaze to Quillon's. "How many are dead?"

The man gave a long sigh. "We don't know. Just hang tight." He walked away, punching at his phone screen.

Cam closed his eyes to shut out the world for a brief moment. He wanted to bawl like a baby and put it down to being overwhelmed and an upcoming adrenaline crash. His heart still pounded like crazy, and his head spun.

The next time he opened his eyes, he stared up into the deepest blue ones. They were reddened and swollen, but they were the most beautiful eyes he'd ever seen.

"Sabrina." His throat was dry, but he managed to croak out her name.

She sniffed. "The paramedics are taking you to the hospital right now. I can't ride with you, but I'm on my way."

He wanted to pull her down for a kiss and reassure her he was okay, but his body wouldn't cooperate. *Shit, why can't I move my arm?*

"We got you splinted, big guy," a disembodied voice stated. "Bullet was a through and through in your tricep but left you with a busted humerus. That's a hard bone to break, so congrats. I hope you're not left-handed."

"We gotta roll!" That call came from someone else.

The paramedic handling Cam waved at someone, then turned back to Sabrina. "Sorry, ma'am, but we need to get outta here. I'll need you to step back."

She swiped her eyes and nodded. "I'll see you soon, Cam."

He had no clue what caused his next action. Hormones or enzymes? Altered brain chemistry?

Emotions running high? It could have been anything or everything. Whatever it was, it bubbled up inside him, filling his chest with such pressure that he had to get it out or burst.

Cam grabbed Sabrina's hand with his uninjured one and blurted out something that had been simmering inside him and now was unstoppable.

"I love you."

19

"What the fuck just happened?"

Baghouse's angered bellow woke Scrap from dozing in his recliner. He shifted himself, trying to find relief from the constant discomfort in his back. The stones he had before were one kind of pain. They started high, then moved with agonizing slowness down through his side and groin until he could pee the damn things out. This pain was different. It stayed in the same place like a nagging wife, never letting up or allowing him any peace.

Scrap inhaled slowly and focused on the chess board sitting on the beat-up table between him and Baghouse. He and his wife came by to check on him, and Mary, of course, decided to cook a meal for them. Scrap had forgotten whose move it was, but it didn't look good for his friend. Checkmate in three moves. If only his life were that simple. Three moves and done. Winner, winner, chicken dinner.

"Did they get the guy? Who's hurt? Where are they now?"

Scrap's brain finally came to full attention and recognized the urgency in Baghouse's questions. *Fuck, something happened.* "What the hell is goin' on?"

Baghouse held up a hand to say he'd explain when he finished his call. "Let me know what they say." He hung up and turned to Scrap with a shocked and haggard face. "That rally the boys planned? Some fucking jagoff turned it into a day for target practice. Eight people shot. One dead, and three in critical. One of our boys went down too. Camshaft caught a bullet while rescuing a kid. Crossman says there's a video blowing up the internet."

Scrap's heart jumped into overdrive, and the pain in his back increased. It took him a moment to process the words. *Rally. Jagoff. Shot. Camshaft.* "Where is he?"

"Hospital with that girl Sabrina. He's been seeing her."

Another pang hit his heart. "Is she okay?" He hoped the gruffness of his voice covered the emotional tempest in his chest.

"Yeah, she was safe. Cross said she kept her cool and helped direct people out of the park."

"You got a Facebook or YouTube thing? Pull up the video."

Someone took the footage with a phone camera, and the picture was shaky, but the angle perfectly captured Cam sprinting toward and scooping up a crying child. The video showed him tucking the little boy into his body, shielding and protecting him as he ran. A couple of shots whizzed by him, the bullets hitting the ground with small dirt explosions. Then Cam jerked and fell, still safeguarding the kid at the peril of his own life. The video stopped with a final picture of Cam covering the boy with his body, leaving his back open and exposed.

"People are commenting on us. How we protect and serve better than the cops. Lotta women saying that's the kind of man they wanna meet." Baghouse took his phone back and slipped it into his back pocket.

Mary bustled out of the kitchen and flipped the drying dish cloth over her shoulder in a practiced move. "I'm not surprised. Camshaft is a very handsome young man who's got his head together."

Scrap shifted uncomfortably, trying to find a position to get some relief. "So? Why the hell should we be concerned about some jagoff's video of Cam getting shot?"

Baghouse gruffed right back at the older man. "Because it makes him a hero. Makes the whole damn club look good too."

"Dammit! Can we erase that shit?"

"Why would you want to do something like that? We've been fading away for years, and before that, people were scared shitless of us. Cam just made us into fucking champions. I expect we'll get some good press out of this. What's wrong with that?"

"That's the problem with expectations," Scrap muttered. "They're always too fucking high."

20

"I'm fuckin' sick of this shit!" Wolf roared.

The rest of the Knights gathered around some hastily set-up card tables at the machine shop. Specs and Stalemate were at the strip club for security until this church meeting ended. The Attic was hopping tonight, full of men with loose wallets drinking up a storm. Money needed to flow, but the club needed privacy for this particular meeting.

The odd addition was Denny, a policeman who happened to be friends with the Knights. Denny followed the law, but he also realized that sometimes justice didn't follow the rules.

Wolf continued to shout. "How the fuck did he get away?"

Ratchet scratched his short dark hair. "I don't know, but I'm sure I winged him. He fell off the back of the shed, out of sight."

Denny tapped his pen on the table's surface. "We got there pretty damn quick. We didn't see a body, but we found a bloodstain on the wall where the fucker slid down." He lifted his head to regard Ratchet. "Nice shot, by the way."

"Thanks."

"Can you match his DNA to some fancy database?" Wolf inquired in a calmer tone.

Denny shook his head. "Only if he's in the system already, but it's not like Hollywood where you have to solve the crime in an hour-long episode. It takes weeks or even months to get answers back on shit like this."

The folding metal chair creaked as Wolf leaned back into it. "So you're saying we're fucked?"

Denny gave a long sigh. "We have the hospitals on alert for GSWs, but there were a number of legit ones that came in from your rally. No telling if one of them was the shooter who simply told the docs he was there as an innocent bystander."

"They have to give names when they check in right? We can take a look at who came in with gunshot wounds and—what?"

Denny's headshake drew everyone's attention. "HIPAA, my friend. We have to have probable cause to get a records warrant. That's gonna be a hard sell to a judge."

"What the fuck can we do about this shit, then?"

"We got our tech guys going through all the videos people posted. We'll piece together what we can and see if we can identify this guy. Chances are, it's part of that duo that's been terrorizing the area."

"Well, it's taking too fucking long!"

Denny's face grew dark. "Look, man, I'm just as frustrated as you are. I'm sick of getting calls to look at another blown-up business or a dead body who used to be a friend and neighbor. Only reason I'm here is to figure this shit out and put a stop to it. If my chief found out I was talking to you bunch, I'd be fired."

Wolf backed down somewhat, but his gold eyes still burned with fire. "Imma do something I never thought I'd do. I'm gonna ask my woman to do a deep dive on the dark net, and yinz already know how I feel about that."

A few of the members squirmed uneasily, and it wasn't because of the uncomfortable chairs. Every one of them remembered how Jazz put herself at risk by hacking into a massive criminal network and nearly lost her life for it. Nowadays, she stuck with her programming app to help protect people from internet scammers. Asking her to go back in was not something Wolf would ever consider unless the situation was desperate.

Denny's grim expression matched the Knights' president's, but they were running out of options. "I get it. I'll back your play as much as I can. How's Cam, by the way?"

"Home. He's got his girl and some high-octane pain pills," Melter informed the group. "I offered him some oxys, but he's got a scrip for percs." He shrugged.

"How the hell do you always have pills?" Crossman asked.

Melter shrugged again. "I have my ways."

Wolf leaned forward. "Please tell me you're not doing pills as well as pot."

Melter let out an affronted scoff. "'Course not! I keep them for other people who might need them. I like my weed. It's natural and organic."

Denny let out a long sigh. "I can't listen to this conversation as I'm not really here, yeah? Just watch yourself, 'cause if you get caught, I'll be the first one to put you in cuffs and throw the book at you." His gaze traveled around the table. "That goes for all of you. I realize that sometimes Lady Justice has her limits, but don't fuck up what yinz forged."

21

Sabrina pulled up to Cam's house, exhausted from a long workday. Maneuvering her bike past the narrow driveway and into the detached two-car garage, she hit the remote to lower the door, popped down her kickstand, and stripped off her lizard helmet. Cam let her borrow his cold gear and gloves, since riding was impossible for him right now. The jacket was loose, but it was still usable. Summer apparently gave up its last hurrah for the rally, and now the weather had turned cold. Rain was forecast again later this week, but she no longer had to worry about her van.

Rugrat and Reptar had their enclosure on the main floor in the dining alcove. Cam added two more rooms to the cage, plus a bigger tree branch.

The beardies greeted her with scampers and waving their hands, begging to be let out for food and pets.

After the park shooting, several businesses stayed closed for extra days, but the massage spa was open for business on Monday morning as usual. Stephan would be out for a few weeks because of his leg injury. He'd lost a lot of blood and had to be rushed through surgery to get the bullet out. According to the ER doctor, he was lucky, as the bullet came close to his femoral artery but didn't damage it. Until he was back on his feet, she and Cicely had to tag-team to keep everything going. It would be a tough couple of months, but they would manage to keep it together somehow.

Rugrat scratched at the bars and stared intently at Sabrina.

"All right, I'm coming," she groused. She opened the door, and both pets scrambled up her arms to sit on her shoulders. "How's Cam today? Sleeping, I hope."

She climbed the twisting staircase carefully so as not to dislodge the two lizards. Sure enough, he was sacked out on a pile of pillows in his boxers, snoring lightly. Straps from the hard white plastic brace graced his bare chest. The device covered his entire upper arm, from shoulder to elbow, restricting his movement and holding everything together. He had to take the thing off once in a while to check the stitched-up bullet wound and clean the area. This was a task best done by her, but not while he slept.

She crept back downstairs, putting the beardies back in their enclosure before heading to the kitchen to check the refrigerator for dinner ingredients. Ground beef, veggies, and potatoes. A half-empty bottle of ketchup sat on the door shelf, and the cabinets held the rest of the ingredients.

Meatloaf coming right up.

She wondered what Scrap was eating in that miserable little house of his.

He'd agreed to go to the health center on Thursday for the checkup that Mary badgered him into and get the DNA test done at the same time. Sabrina had asked Cicely for that hour off to go with him. It wasn't like she had any obligations to the man, but decent people helped others, right?

She dumped the meat, spices, and breadcrumbs into a mixing bowl and squirted a generous amount of ketchup over the pile. As she pressed it all together, she thought about cooking enough dinner for three and borrowing Cam's truck to take some over to Scrap's place. Chances were that he was home, as he rarely left it since his fall. It wasn't that far either.

Her mind wandered through various topics as she worked. This was Cam's house, yet she'd already learned where everything was, and he'd let her rearrange stuff as she wanted. The beardies had their new palace, and Cam had mentioned clearing out one of the extra bedrooms and setting up a home spa kind of place in case she wanted to take on some private work. More and more, their lives were becoming integrated.

The woman who never quite fit in had found a space where she slotted in so comfortably, it snuck up on her how perfect it felt to be here.

She liked it. She liked it a lot.

Sabrina smiled to herself as she opened the fridge again to take out an egg for the meat mixture. She was so far into her thoughts, it startled her when a knock sounded at the front door. Thinking it was one of the Knights coming to check on Cam, she darted forward to answer it before they knocked again and woke him up.

She would forever regret not checking the peephole first.

Raquel stood on the covered porch. She lowered

her sunglasses to peer over the frames at her daughter. "Hi, Sabrina. It's been a while."

Shock coursed through Sabrina's body. Not the good kind like when Cam kissed her or said he loved her. They still hadn't talked about that yet, as he'd been in a hazy drug stupor since she brought him home Saturday night. No, this jolt made her heart jump into overtime fight-or-flight instinct. This was Cam's place, and it was now hers too. Sabrina had never been one to run from a conflict, so fight it was.

"What the hell are you doing here?"

"Invite me in and I'll tell you."

It was on the tip of Sabrina's tongue to tell the woman to fuck off and leave, but she couldn't bring herself to do it. She didn't fool herself into thinking Raquel showed up from any maternal drive. Was it money, like always, or something else? Curiosity won, and Sabrina stepped back to allow entrance.

The click from Raquel's heels echoed in the open space as she walked across the wood floor. Her jeans were tight across her small butt and rode low on nonexistent hips. The leather jacket was new but had no patches to say if she still belonged to a biker group.

Time had left its mark on the older woman, but she was still stunning in appearance. Black, blonde, and red streaks highlighted her hair, and she'd carefully applied her heavy makeup to hide her age. She lifted the sunglasses onto her head in a practiced motion. "So, how've you been?"

Really? "Do you mean recently, or since the last time I saw you, when I was eighteen?" Sabrina packed the meat into a loaf pan and slipped it into the oven. No way was she planning to invite the woman for dinner. "How did you know I was here?"

Raquel ignored the dig and sat down on the sofa, crossing her legs as if settling in for a long visit. "I got sources. Word is, Rodrigo went off about you at some party. Said you were in Pennsylvania dealing with a dying father. I put two and two together and came up with Pittsburgh." She scanned the room with her deep blue eyes and smirked as she leaned back against the cushions. "Seems you've landed on your feet." She examined the coffin-shaped nails on one hand. Their ruby color reminded Sabrina of blood. "Then again, you always did. Got yourself a man with some money. Good for you."

"Again, why are you here, Raquel?" Sabrina couldn't bring herself to call the woman *mother*.

Raquel raised a sculpted eyebrow. "To make sure you get your fair share of your father's estate."

"Ernie died without leaving a will. Rodrigo is his

official son. Case closed." Sabrina wiped her hands as she turned her back and walked over to the lizard condo. Her knees locked as she pulled a bag of freeze-dried crickets from the shelf under the reptile cage complex. "Rodrigo already called me about it, and I told him to fuck off. I don't have the time to deal with that right now."

Raquel sneered and flipped a handful of multi-colored hair over her shoulder. "That kid was always a little shit. Ernie adopted him just before he married me. Rosa put that idea in his head. She and Julia, Roddie's mom, were best friends, and when Julia died, Rosa convinced Ernie to take him in, then practically took over raising him herself. You'd have thought *she* was his mom with the way she doted on him, always coming over to spend time with him. That bitch never did like me and didn't want me anywhere near him."

Surprise, surprise! "I'm aware. Aunt Rosa doesn't like anyone but Rodrigo."

Raquel gave a short laugh. "When you came along, Ernie was thrilled to have a bio-baby, even with the different eyes and coloring. I never said anything to him to make him think differently. It was Rosa who poisoned him with her shit about Rodrigo being his 'true son.'" She tossed her head back. "It doesn't matter, 'cause either way, you're sitting real pretty right now. There's a pile of money just waiting for you if you play your cards right."

"Did you miss the part where I said Ernie died without a will? I have no plans to put myself in between Rodrigo and whatever estate my dad left behind." Sabrina sprinkled a handful of the insects into the cage. Reptar and Rugrat scrambled down the tree branches to grab them.

Raquel huffed and rolled her eyes under the thick fake lashes. "You don't get it, do you? I'm not talking about just Ernie."

Cold dread hit her gut and spread out to rest in her bones. Raquel was up to something. She wouldn't be here otherwise. The familiar helpless feeling Sabrina remembered as a child came back and sat on her like a heavy wet blanket. "Which father are you talking about?"

"Truthfully, I'm not sure. It could be Ernie, but there's a good chance it's Scrap."

Sabrina's stomach flipped and twisted so hard, she had to grab the cage's frame to stay upright. She imagined the stains left behind by the flying blood and gore from her exploded head. She was losing patience. "I wish you would just spit it out and quit messing around."

"You're not stupid." Raquel's purr sounded almost as reptilian as the beardies. "As Walter's only child, you get *all* of his money. That stingy rat bastard has assets no one knows about. Not just the titty bar, but even that is gold. You'd be one rich cookie. All's we have to do is get the DNA results and you'll be set."

Sabrina hardly believed her ears, and yet she wasn't surprised by her mother's vulturelike attitude. "Scrap ain't dead. How do you know all this?"

"Like I said, I got sources. Ones that told me he's in bad shape and it's only a matter of time. That man has one leg and half the other in the grave. There's no way he'll do dialysis or anything like that. Unless, by some chance, he gets a kidney, I don't expect he'll be around for another year."

Sabrina whirled around from the cage to face the woman who gave birth to her and little else. "What if we're a match? What if I decide to give him one of mine?"

The older woman's eyes narrowed to slits. "Why the hell would you do that?"

"Oh, I don't know. How 'bout being a decent human being?"

"Ha!" Raquel tossed her hair back in a habitual

flip. "That man has never done a damn thing for anyone. He doesn't deserve it."

Pot, meet kettle!

Sabrina opened her mouth to blast her mother when she got interrupted.

"What's going on?"

The male voice cut through the air like ice. Sabrina turned to see Cam standing at the bottom of the spiral stairs. He leaned to one side and had his good arm raised with his fingertips clutching the railing, his other arm hanging in its cast at his side. Laser beams aimed straight for Raquel shot from his eyes, and Sabrina had no doubt he heard her comment.

"Nothing except your girl here wants to give a big piece of her body to her dad." Raquel clicked her talons together at Sabrina.

"Number one, we don't know if Scrap is her father yet. Number two, it's her choice what she does with her body. And number three—" He took two steps into the room. "—none of this is your business, period."

Raquel hummed a little laugh. "It's my business if he never updated his will."

A low buzz started in Sabrina's ears, that mystery

vibration when something bad is coming. "What are you saying?"

The Cheshire grin on Raquel's face showed her exact meaning. "Ernie didn't leave a will. We could still make a claim and get something from his estate. If Scrap dies, he named us both as his heirs but named you as the primary. He told me he planned to cut me out, but he was always bad about following up. No matter what, I bet he kept your name in his will, just in case. If he never changed it again, you could still be in it. And even if he did, the will might not even be legal if he didn't get it notarized and filed, so there's a good chance I still might be named somewhere as executor. We'll sell it all and split everything down the middle, any property, assets, insurance policies, and whatever else he has. That includes Attic and his part of the machine shop. We'll sell everything and walk away."

Sabrina's breath whooshed out of her as if she'd been punched in the gut. "Who the hell do you think you are? I swear, you're like a vampire hovering over her victim, ready to suck out every drop of blood she can. We're not splitting anything." She shook her head. "What am I saying? Fuck!" She clenched two fists at her temples. "I can't handle this right now."

Luckily, she didn't have to.

"Get the fuck outta my house, and do not come back." Cam's menacing tone was low but forceful.

Raquel ignored him. "Scrap has some serious money he hides from everyone. You could be rich, Sabrina."

Visions of a harpy with Raquel's face picking over the dead corpses of Ernie and Scrap burst behind Sabrina's eyes. "You know what? My man said get the fuck out, and he meant it."

Raquel squinted at her with a nasty smile. "He's got a broken arm. What are you gonna do, daughter? Call the cops?"

"No," Sabrina snapped. "I'm gonna call the Iron City Knights. I bet they'll get here faster."

For the first time, Raquel faltered. Her mouth turned down and her eyes dropped to the floor. "Doesn't matter. Walter is on his way out, and if he never redid his will, there's nothing you or the Knights can do about it. I plan on taking what's coming to me."

"Are you deaf?" Sabrina asked in a rigid voice. She turned to Cam. "I think she's deaf. Maybe I should give her a sign." She twisted back to face Raquel and raised her middle finger. "How 'bout this one?"

"You're gonna regret not working with me," Raquel sneered. "I'll force you and the club to sell every asset he has. I can put the court on my side."

"Yeah, baby, I think she is deaf." Cam let go of the railing and strode forward. "Yeah, I got a bum arm, but I only need one to toss you out."

"No need, sweetcakes," Raquel purred. "I'm leaving." As she sashayed to the door, she paused. "Think about it, right?"

The click of the front door closing triggered an explosive exhale from Sabrina. "I can't believe her! Who does that shit?" She pulled from her anger, mostly to keep herself from collapsing to the floor. Agitation sparked down her legs, and she had to start moving or go insane. She stomped around in a circle, laying down heavy steps and throwing her arms out wildly; if she slowed down, she'd fall into a big pile of tears. Sarcasm flowed freely in her words. "Good afternoon, Cam. That was Raquel, a vampire who sucks the life out of everyone around her. Bonus round—she gave birth to *moi*!"

Her pacing quickly slowed as her anger burned out and gave way to a smoldering in her gut. "Why the hell are you interested in me?" She stopped her frantic movements and stared at the man who stood and watched her in silence. "I'm about as fucked up as you can get. I've got a possible father who is stubborn as hell, mean as a snake, and refuses to acknowledge me. And I've got a mother who could win medals if the Olympics had a selfish, greedy, and opportunistic category."

Tears formed and finally flowed. She couldn't hold it back any longer. Once they started, they wouldn't stop. "Dammit, I hate crying. So fucking useless." She sniffed and wiped at her tears, jerking her hand across her face to dash away the offending wetness. "I miss my dad."

Then Cam was there. He folded her under his one good arm, pulling her in tight and placing a layer of comfort around her like a warm blanket. "I got you. No one is here but you and me. The beardies, too, but they won't judge either."

Safe.

She felt safe.

Safe enough to let go.

She cried. Long. Hard. Unceasing. All the pent-up emotions burst out of her from years of forcing them behind a dam of concrete control.

She cried for the child who was abandoned by her mother.

She cried for the teenager who never got accepted by the only family she had.

She cried for the loss of her dad who died and left her on her own.

She cried for the rejection of her possible father.

As much as she put up the rough-and-tough exterior, inside there was a person who needed to be loved and accepted somewhere by someone.

Gradually, her sobs subsided, and she calmed. Cam held her through the storm, rubbing her back and murmuring over and over again, "I got you. I got you, babe."

She let go of the death grip on his shirt. "I'm sorry I lost it."

"Don't ever be sorry for being human, sweetheart. You don't get to grow up without some baggage coming along for the ride."

She pulled back and swiped at her face. "I'm probably blotchy as hell. I'm gonna rinse myself and finish dinner for us."

"How 'bout you go rinse yourself and *I'll* finish dinner for us?"

She gave him a skeptical side-eye. "You sure you can handle that?"

He raised his plastic cast. "I can manage. Not my first time with a busted arm."

She sniffed and dragged a finger under her nose. "I won't argue. I'm all snotty and stuffy. I hate that."

"Me too. Go do your thing, baby. We'll talk more later, yeah?"

"Okay."

Sabrina used the half bath on the main floor to wash her face, then made some toilet-paper compresses with cold water to put on her eyes. The mirror told her she had the raccoon thing going on, but she didn't worry too much about it. If Cam wanted a glamour model at all times, he would be disappointed, but he didn't seem to mind. Real life didn't always appear perfect and put together. Sometimes it came with snot and smeared makeup.

Nuked baked potatoes, steamed veggies, and a nice, firm meatloaf awaited her when she returned a few minutes later.

"Wanna talk about it?" he asked while juggling plates from the cabinet.

"Not really." She pulled cutlery from the drawer. "Is it weird to want a regular dinner and conversation after all the shit that just got dumped on our doorstep?"

He grinned. "I like how you said 'our.' And yeah, this whole deal is weird, but we'll figure it all out. I don't know squat about the legal side of things, but nothing will happen on any front until we know for sure if you're Scrap's daughter or not."

They sat at the bar with loaded plates. "You got any thoughts about how to deal with Raquel?" Cam asked.

Sabrina poked at her veggies. "I have no idea where she's staying or when she'll turn up again. This is her pattern—showing up at the most inconvenient, random times and stirring up shit."

He put his fork down and turned to face her with a serious expression. "I got one of those too. My foster sister, Tammie, is back in town. She and Raquel could be twins."

"You've mentioned her before."

"Yeah." His eyes went back to his plate, and he lifted his fork to prod at the meatloaf. "This is really good."

Sabrina's radar pinged. "What aren't you telling me?"

Cam breathed deeply, as if debating. "I think we've had enough bullshit to handle tonight. I'll tell you about it some other time, yeah? Right now, I'm ready for some dessert."

She blinked. "I'm sorry, sugar. I didn't make anything."

He grinned at her. "Oh, I have something sweet in mind."

22

Fatigue and exasperation showed on every Knight's face at the church meeting. They were now held daily at the machine shop. Quillon didn't like it much, as it disturbed his business, but it was simpler to stop production for an hour there rather than kick patrons out of the titty bar.

Cam tried to concentrate on the discussion, but his mind kept wandering back to the previous night and the turning point connection he'd made with Sabrina. She truly belonged to him now, hook, line, and sinker. After dinner, he took her upstairs, where he made her come again and again. He licked his lips as he remembered her flavor and the sounds she made just before she orgasmed. He did it with his mouth for the first round, and then she climbed on top and rode him for the second. Her breasts moved naturally as she ground herself on his cock, taking him far inside her depths. The cast made it awkward, but it didn't stop him from adding his own thrusts. She demanded it hard and fast, solidly in the driver's seat as she took the lead and brought them both to complete fulfillment.

Quillon rapped his knuckles on the table, breaking into Cam's erotic daydream. He leaned forward to hide the partial erection in his jeans and brought himself back to the business at hand.

"The rally raised a nice sum for the Hob family despite the shooter. Tracie and I took a check over to Mira, and she cried all over us. Said she's gonna move to Fieldale, Virginia, some little town where her mom lives. There's more family support for her and the kids there. She's selling the business, or at least the tools and contents. Few people go into shoe repair anymore. Damn shame."

Wolf grunted as he shifted on his metal chair. "That's some good news, at least. Let her know we're available if she needs bodies to help her get squared away and packed up." His eyes roamed the table. "Specs says there are four women who won Date Knights. You boys get those set up ASAP."

Specs nodded animatedly, like a bobblehead

Funko toy. "I have all of their contact information in a spreadsheet. Make sure I have everyone's email and I'll send the details later."

"Do we get to fuck them?" Ratchet grinned.

Cam cursed under his breath. Ratchet had a one-track mind that always led to a bedroom, or at least a blow job.

Melter snorted. "Did you get the fat one?"

Ratchet jerked his head. "Hey, man, I don't mind a little more cushion for the pushin'. Just aim for the wet spot and ride the waves."

Wolf's eyebrows came together in irritation. "Don't be an asshole, ya jagoff. That's up to the woman. She wants to fuck, have at it, but you make damn sure if it's a one-time thing, she knows it. If she doesn't want to fuck or has a problem with a one-nighter, you better show some respect and leave her alone. Take her out and be a gentleman, understood? We got eyes on us now because of that video of Cam going viral. More customers at the titty bar asking about joining us. More women coming around to check us out. We got people greeting us on the streets now, like old friends. We do not want to fuck this up."

Ratchet's face fell a bit, but he nodded his agreement. "Got it, boss."

Wolf tapped his fingers on the table. "I heard Raquel is back. Does Scrap know?"

Baghouse squirmed under the club's scrutiny. He locked eyes with Cam and let out a long sigh. "Yeah, he knows. Bitch called him a few days ago." He hesitated, then sighed again. "I might as well tell everyone. Scrap isn't doing too good. He's got... fuck... he's gonna lose his shit for me saying this, but yinz will find out anyway. He's got kidney disease. He's been diabetic for years but never did anything to take care of it, and now he's paying that price. His kidneys are shot, and he's looking at long-term dialysis or a transplant."

A jolt hit Cam's gut as the rest of the Knights learned what their founder dealt with these days. Now that the news was out, collective whistles and curses circled the tables. Scrap might be the most cantankerous man to deal with in the club, but he was still a member and a former president.

Wolf took a breath and stilled his moving hand. "Cam? Has anything been confirmed about him and Sabrina being related?

"Not yet. Supposed to happen soon, though. Maybe a week or two."

Wolf grunted an acknowledgment but continued with the agenda. "Keep us informed, yeah?" He lifted his hand and jammed it over his face. "Christ on a cracker. I've been talking with Denny regularly about shit going down. He's updated us, but the problem is, he doesn't have anything different. I asked him about the cop patrols, and he said he would hold off for a few days, but if one more business gets firebombed, he's gonna be up our asses every day."

Cam hated the idea of police trolling the area, but if the Knights couldn't keep their promise of protection, then few options remained.

Wolf's appearance was haggard and full of fatigue. Cam bet the president wasn't sleeping too well right now, and he couldn't blame the man. He carried a heavy weight on those broad shoulders.

They only needed one break. One clue. One piece of information that would lead them to the jagoffs who'd already hurt so many people and killed two.

His eyes roamed the table and landed on Specs. The man had a weird grin on his face. Cam found it strange, but Specs was strange anyway. Still, it wasn't appropriate given the topic. "Yo, Specs. What's so funny?"

The man jumped as he was called out, eyes wide behind his thick glasses. "Oh... um... nothing. I was thinking 'bout Ratchet and his date. I guess he'll have to modify his suspension for that size woman."

"Didn't I just say something about showing some respect?" Wolf growled.

Specs dropped his eyes like a good beta. "Sorry, sir."

Cam wasn't happy about it either, but there was a lot happening, and all the Knights needed to be on the same page. It bothered him that Baghouse, a senior member, would keep the news of Scrap's failing health to himself for so long, but he figured the man had his reasons. It bothered him, too, that the older Knights had purposely hidden their lives outside of the club. Maybe it was a privacy thing, but his strong belief was if the Iron City Knights were to become a solid group, they needed to start with brotherhood and forge trust between themselves. That meant if one member was sick, they rallied around for support. If another member needed help in whatever form that required, they showed up with working hands. If someone was in trouble with the law, they would break a few to protect one another.

The meeting was dismissed with no resolutions or progress. Ratchet made a few more sex jokes, but no one laughed. Stalemate caught Cam's attention with his stoic expression. That man was colder than ice and had the emotional equivalent of a rock. If his "date" had any expectations of a bright future with him, they would be dashed in a heartbeat.

Cam's phone buzzed, and he swore softly when he spotted the name. Heading off to the side, away from the others, he answered. "Now is not a good time, Tammie."

"Iz id ever a good time?" The drunken voice laughed at the other end of the connection. "I won't bodder you again. Promise. I jus' need a liddle help to get m'self to-gedder. I'll pay you back."

"That's what you said the last time."

She grumbled before saying, "Times are hard, ya know?"

He closed his eyes as he walked to his bike. "How much?"

"Can I ged two thousand?"

"No."

"How 'bout fifteen hun'erd?"

His fingers came up to pinch the bridge of his nose. "How 'bout five hundred?"

"Five hun'erd won't pay my rent!"

It was hard to tell if her outrage was real or manufactured. "I'm not giving you any more money. Tell me where you're staying and I'll pay the rent this month."

"Doan' need that. I need muney!"

"The most I'll do for you is pay your rent."

She cursed and hung up. Cam closed the screen on his phone and tucked it into his back pocket with shaking hands. This was not the first time she'd called him for money and probably wouldn't be the last.

The familiar helplessness washed over him. Urges to fix his sister coupled with the knowledge that there wasn't a damn thing he could do about this situation. He didn't know where he was on the list, before or after his foster brothers, but Tammie would hit them up too. Rehab had been a condition once, and to her credit, she'd tried it and stayed clean for a few months, but it didn't last.

On impulse, he pulled out his phone again and dialed Sabrina.

"Hey, sugar. What's up?"

Her bright voice brought an instant relief to his troubled mind. "Got any free time this afternoon?"

"You mean for an appointment? Hold on."

Clicking keys told him she was at the front desk looking up the spa calendar. "Yup. My three o'clock canceled. If you want to come see me here, that's fine, but I can do you at home later."

Home. He loved hearing that word come from her lips. "I need you now."

"Sure, sweetheart. See you in a bit."

Cam Ubered to Sunstone Healing, as his arm wasn't healed enough to ride. The bookstore was nothing more than a burnt-out shell, making it an eyesore in the strip of businesses. Crossman told him in private that Brianna's insurance claims were met with resistance from the company and she also had a lot of grief in her home life. He talked about the girl a lot, and it seemed that he had an interest in the bookstore owner. Cam wished them both well.

An ashy smell still permeated the air as he walked into the spa. Cicely stood at the counter, examining her short nails with their bright pink polish. She gave him an obvious fake smile. "She'll be done with her client in about twenty minutes. I can do you."

"I'll wait."

The woman's smile dropped, and she huffed, "Suit yourself."

Cam sat down in one of the chairs and did his best

not to replay the short phone conversation he'd just had with Tammie. It was the same one, repeated every so often when his past came back to haunt him. He thought he'd slain those demons, but every once in a while, he'd have to pull out his sword and do it again.

After getting off the phone with her, he needed some fresh air and a long ride, but not with his arm still in a cast. When spring came around, he planned to load up his gear and take Sabrina on a long camping trip. He pictured the two of them riding the Allegheny National Forest Loop or exploring Amish country around Lancaster. As he sat in the waiting area, he hoped his plans worked out. At the present, his emotions had his shoulders in knots and his legs so tight they hurt. He thought about the relief her hands could bring him. His need for this was so tangible, he had to force himself to sit still.

A blonde woman bounced down the hallway, all grins and giggles. "I feel soooo good now! Two weeks?"

"I got it." Sabrina appeared right behind her, and Cam felt his back easing a bit just from seeing her. She waved at him and winked. That one gesture made everything right in his world. At least for now.

Sabrina presented the terminal for the woman to tap her card and confirmed the regular appointment. Cam admired the professional way she handled herself. Their relationship was still budding, and he wanted to see a full bloom soon. In order for that to happen, all cards had to be on the table. Would this be the best time?

He hoped so.

"You got the energy for one more today?"

She arched a brow and gave him direct eye contact. "I'll always have energy for you, sugar. Come on back. We'll have to make accommodations for the cast. How 'bout we try the chair instead of the table?"

"You're the expert."

It didn't take long for her to set up the different apparatus and leave the room so he could strip. Hopefully, his boxer briefs were okay. He situated himself on the padded seat. Her soft knock came just as he put his face in the donut cradle.

"What are we working on today?" She straightened the top sheet, smoothing her hands over his back.

Just that one touch had him relaxing. "All over, I guess."

"Can you be more specific?"

"My shoulders are killing me, and my neck is really stiff."

"Okay, sugar. Let me know if it's too much."

The dig of her thumbs into his deltoids hurt like hell but felt good at the same time. The clean scent of the room and the ethereal background music helped him drowse into a better mood.

"So, what's got you worked up, sugar?"

He really didn't want to give her that answer, not when he was under her hands and she was releasing all the tension in his muscles. But he needed to warn her before she was put in a really bad spot.

"I got a call today." He took a breath and let it out slowly. "From my sister, Tammie."

Her hands stopped on the small of his back. "I'm guessing this didn't make you happy?"

"No, it did not. I'm telling you this in case she shows up at the house. If she does and I'm not there, under no circumstances do you let her in. Got it? Whatever sob story she tells you, keep her out and call me or the police."

Sabrina pressed into a tight tendon near his lower spine near the tattooed words "Start over." "Oh. Okay."

"Are you going to ask me why?"

She moved to another spot on the same tendon. "No, sugar, I'm not gonna ask. If you want to share, though, I'll listen. I think you already know how fucked up my family situation is. Not much is gonna shock and bother me."

"You might be surprised. Not everyone knows my story. Wolf heard part of it when we were hanging out one night. I don't drink very often, but we were celebrating Quillon and Tracie's wedding, and I had one too many and shared too much."

Sabrina stroked her oiled hands over his obliques, and he breathed as she released more of his tension with the firm movement. "You can tell me or not, Cam. I swear I'm not going to judge you."

Where do I start? "Well, you know I grew up in a foster home. My real mom was a serial drug addict and a part-time hooker. She had no clue who my father was. I guess I'm grateful that she tried to stop using while she was pregnant with me, but she fell off the wagon several times before I was born. I spent the first weeks of my life in a NICU as a preemie and going through withdrawal. By all accounts, I should have had more problems, but somehow I avoided a lot of the crack-baby issues."

"I'm glad you overcame that." She continued to work, sliding her fingers under his armpit and pressing into the front tendon at his right pectoral. The burn helped keep his focus. "Where is she now?"

"No idea. She might be in prison or dead. I don't remember much of her, just the smell of cigarettes and being hungry. If she's still alive and I saw her on the street, I wouldn't recognize her. I spent some time getting shuffled around from place to place, in and out of the children's home, not knowing where I might sleep next."

"That's really rough, sugar. I'm glad you found Vera and Cecil when you did."

Cam fell silent for a minute or two and concentrated on Sabrina's touch. She smoothed over his back and shoulders before seating herself on a rolling stool. After gently positioning his right forearm, she began to tackle the knots at his elbow. "Their house was the haven I needed. They took me in and treated me like a son. Kyle and Morgan were older and already there. We were more like friends than brothers, but it was okay. We had a family and parents who taught us how it's supposed to be." He took a breath. "Then Tammie came into our lives."

The tendon released, and Sabrina shifted to work on his hand. "I get the feeling this wasn't a good thing?"

"At first we all thought it was. Tammie's a year younger than me and was one grade below me when we were in school. I was a sophomore when she came to live with us. Kyle was a senior and Morgan still lived there while he went to community college, so we still had a full house. Tammie... Tammie was... damaged."

"I see. Is this something you want... need to share? I'll listen if that's what you want."

He nodded. "Tammie was also born to an addict and had a lot of problems as a kid. More than I did. She spent more time than me getting bounced around between living with her mom and living in foster homes. When she moved in with us, it was good for a while, but then it wasn't. It got bad. Real bad."

"I'm sorry." The stool squeaked as she rolled to his left side and repeated the massage, minus the arm. "Did your foster parents send her back to the children's home?"

"Not at first. They felt they were the last hope Tammie had. Fuck, they tried so damn hard, but Tammie was a master at manipulation. She broke every rule they had, then turned around and begged for forgiveness. Cuss at Vera, then turn on the waterworks and say she was sorry. She started staying out way past curfew, sometimes drinking, then would cry and hug them until they let her back in. They tried to overlook her problems and work with her, but she wasn't having it. It took a couple years before we reached the last straw and gave up."

A sharp rap came at the door before Cicely poked in her head. "I'm finished for the day. I'll lock the front. Do some cleaning before you leave."

"Sure. I'll see you tomorrow."

Cicely closed the door in silence. No "thank you" or "you too" passed her lips.

"What's wrong with her?" Cam asked.

Sabrina sighed heavily. "I don't know. She's constantly on my case about something. I'm assuming it's because we're down a person and the overtime is getting to her." She finished his hand and shifted to stand behind him. "It sounds like Tammie needed help, but not the kind your parents could give her."

"I thought the same thing for a long time, but you know, at some point, people have to take responsibility and not put the blame for their problems on others. Maybe I'm not being fair, but when she...."

He fell silent. This was harder than he thought. Tears formed in his eyes, hidden from view by the head cradle.

Sabrina placed her hands on his shoulders and stroked the back of his neck with her thumbs. "Must be something pretty radical if it still affects you like this. You don't have to tell me if it's too much."

"I'm afraid you'll look at me with different eyes."

She stilled at his words. "I think you can tell I'm a pretty tough person. My life hasn't exactly been all rosy perfect either." She paused. "You asked me once about taking a chance on you. How 'bout you take a chance on me?"

He took a breath as she resumed the massage on the back of his neck. It felt more like a caress now. "I'd graduated from high school, but my parents let me stay in the house while I went to community college for machining and design. My girlfriend, Caitlin, was there working on her accounting degree. Tammie hated her. Of course, she hated everyone and everything."

"How old was she?"

"Seventeen. Almost eighteen, so yeah, the teenager mindset didn't help, but when I say she hated everything, I mean she *hated* it. She used to fly into these uncontrollable rages where she would throw whatever she could lay her hands on. Screaming at the top of her lungs. Cursing. Kicking. Punching. You wouldn't believe the shit she destroyed. Furniture. Dishes. Vera had this nice collection of Hummel figurines that got smashed during one episode. They tried doctors and counselors, then medication that Tammie refused to take. I spent a lot of time at Caitlin's place, but I still needed to be at home to protect my parents. Make sense?"

"I get it. I thought I'd feel sorry for Tammie, but she sounds like a little witch."

He sighed. "I don't know. Part of me blames her rotten childhood, but when does that just become an excuse?"

"Deep subject." Sabrina's fingers traced over his skull, scratching his scalp lightly with her nails. "One I'm not gonna speculate about. No one can see what's going on in someone else's head."

Cam liked the head massage. "One night, I was at the house having dinner with Vera and Cecil. Tammie was supposed to come home after school. I hung out until she finally showed up. At three in the morning. Cecil had gone to bed, but Vera and I stayed up dozing in the living room. Tammie came in stinking of booze and sex. She was high or drunk or both. Some of the shit that spewed out of her mouth...."

His voice faded as his memories took over. "She told me she wanted to fuck me. That she would be so much better than Caitlin."

He paused, images of that night coming back to him. "She ignored Vera, who sat right next to me on the sofa, and came over to... mount me. She tried to kiss me and hump me, telling me how good she could be. She grabbed for my dick, and I shoved her off me. I wasn't nice about it either."

Sabrina's hands slowed. "That sounds really intense."

"That's one way of putting it. I told her *that* would never happen and she needed to straighten up her act. She got mad, of course, and threw one of the flower vases at me, then kicked the coffee table until it broke into pieces. Vera tried to stop her, and Tammie went wild. She started slapping and punching Vera in the face. I still remember Tammie's nails digging into my mom's cheeks and the blood from those wounds. I shoved Tammie out of the way and shielded Vera with my body. I yelled for her to stop, but she was so out of control, I don't know if she heard me. To this day, I have no clue why she didn't stop. Either she couldn't or she wouldn't."

Sabrina's arms came around him in a hug, her body pressing into his back. "I'm so sorry you had to go through that. I'm sorry for Vera and Cecil too. I'm not sure about Tammie."

"It's not over." Cam swallowed the huge lump in

his throat. What would Sabrina think of him now? "Tammie picked up one of the broken table legs and started hitting me. It had jagged pieces on it, plus a few nails. It tore into me and ripped open my back as I was covering Vera. The fucking pain got to me. I... fuck... I lost it and hit my sister. Twice. Punched her right in the face. Dropped her like a stone. The cops said it was self-defense all the way, but—"

The sob caught him off guard. It took him a minute to figure out it came from his own mouth. Speech was impossible now.

Sabrina held him from behind, allowing him the courtesy of keeping his face hidden in the cradle. He appreciated that gesture, but he wished he could see her face to guess at what she thought about him now.

"I was almost six feet tall and over two hundred pounds of muscle. Tammie was five foot four and around one-twenty-five. I could have hurt her real bad. The first punch was to get her off me and my mom. The second... I think the second was from years of frustration and anger. It shames me."

She placed her chin on his shoulder. "You ever hit another woman?"

"No. Never."

Her breath tickled his neck as she spoke. "I

believe you, and I bet I can guess what happened next. Lots of charges were made and some of them dropped. Caitlin broke up with you. Tammie was removed and sent to juvie."

"Yes."

"Why did Vera and Cecil keep Tammie in their will?"

He sniffed back his tears. "I think it's because she was the last one in their care and the only one they failed to help. On her deathbed, Vera asked Morgan, Kyle, and me to look after her. We still do, but I'll be honest, I resent it. She never got clean. Since juvie, she's been in and out of jail for a lot of things. Solicitation, shoplifting, assault."

He paused. There were hundreds more stories about Tammie over the years. Ones the movies never quite got it right as to how bad those situations were in reality. It made confessing his true feelings hard to do, and he'd kept them bottled up for years. He suspected it was the same with his foster brothers, but none of them had dared say the words out loud until now.

"I hate her. I hate my sister for what she did to my parents and what she did to me."

If there was a stronger word than hate, he would have used it. Loathe. Abhor. Detest. Some other description of the total disgust he felt when he dealt with Tammie. He recognized that she was a broken person, but the ugly in her made it impossible to see anything else. He didn't have it in him to forgive his foster sister, even though he still helped her.

Sabrina kissed his neck. "We make a pair, don't we? Both of us had sucky moms, both of us had nasty siblings, both of us are estranged from family. You let me cry it out, and now I'm letting you do the same. I vote to be done with other people's bullshit. We'll make our own life and family. I've decided it's worth it for me to stay here and be a part of this community. It doesn't matter about Scrap and me or Rodrigo's shit or Tammie. I'm gonna stick."

"Think you'll ever be afraid of me?"

She laughed. He wasn't expecting that reaction, and it startled him.

"Not in this lifetime, sugar. Now, let's go home. If you want, I'll let you be on top this time."

23

Jazz flexed her fingers and stretched her arms. She sat at her home computer desk, which looked like a command center in one of her favorite sci-fi movies. She'd expanded it to three monitors and customized everything with extra components that her friend and mentor, Copperpot100, told her about. The speed was off the charts and enhanced her hacking abilities to something the government might jail her for having.

"Here goes nothing," she said under her breath as she wrapped her blue hair into a ponytail and placed her hands on the keyboard.

"Why are you whispering, babe?" Wolf's voice boomed in the open room.

Jazz jumped with a cry. *"Yah!* Don't do that!"

He laughed and came behind her to check out the windows she had open on the screens. "No one's here but you, me, and Freya." He nuzzled her neck. "You need to take a break?"

Don't start something you can't finish. Stop messing with me right now. "Don't stop messing." *Argh!* "I mean finish me now." She rolled her eyes at her mixed-up words and took a breath to center herself. "This is important, right? Show some respect for the process."

He chuckled and pulled up a chair. "Mind if I watch?"

"As long as you stay silent and just observe. Otherwise, go away."

"I'll be quiet."

The construction workers completed their house last week, and they'd moved into the new digs as soon as the paint dried. The new design had an open floor plan with big windows and an extended deck to watch the Allegheny River flow by. Right now, Jazz wasn't looking at anything other than the wall of computer power in front of her.

She took a sip of herbal tea from her unicorn mug and placed her fingers on the keyboard. They flew over the tiny squares in rapid motion, never stopping or faltering. Images came up on the triple screens—angles from different security cameras belonging to neighboring businesses, CCTV, and even some car dashcams. She zoomed in and out with dizzying speed, looking at reflections and shadows, license plates on cars parked on the surrounding streets where each incident took place, and even hacked into the cell videos taken during the rally. Many had been posted on social media, but nothing got the viral hits like the one showing Cam's rescue of the child. Jazz enhanced that video until she could see the blood splatter from where Cam was shot. Then she noticed a person in the corner of the screen, filming the incident from the front angle.

"Look at that." She pointed to the figure and zoomed in, enhancing and filling in pixels for clarity. "That woman took a video from the other side. Maybe she got a piece of the back part, where the shooter was on top of that building."

Wolf perked up at that. "Can you find that video?"

Jazz continued to type as she searched. "I have to identify her first. I have a facial recognition program that should find—there. She's employed by Marty's Sweets over in Cannonsburg. Ooh, lookie! She entered the Date Knight contest with a hundred tickets. Looks like she won Melter."

"The video, babe. Can you find the video?"

"I'm getting into her phone to see. This one has a tough firewall, but I'll find the chink in the armor."

Wolf raised an eyebrow at the contents of the computer screens. "I'm impressed and a little scared of you right now."

Jazz grinned and took another sip of tea as the woman's phone information loaded. "As long as I never have a reason to do a deep dive on you, you're safe."

He pulled her attention away from the monitors by cupping her chin and turning her head to his for a quick kiss. "That, I can guarantee. By the way, your brother came by earlier today."

Her face lit up with delight as she turned back to her work. "What did Hugo have to say about the new digs?"

"He wanted to know when his room would be ready."

"Ha! Like he would ever leave his place at the group home. He's surrounded by other adults with Down syndrome and loves working at the dog treat company. What more could he ask for?"

"I still want him to remember that he always has a place with us if he ever needs or wants it. I told him he could pick out what he wants to decorate a room here with so he's always move-in ready."

"Oooh, you're makin' me all gooey inside," she gushed. "I can't concentrate when you do that!"

Wolf laughed, then went quiet again as Jazz rummaged through pictures and videos on the woman's phone. Scene after scene flashed by for several minutes. "Oh! Here we go!"

There were multiple pictures of Cam in addition to a video of him getting shot. The angle wasn't the best, but the storage building the shooter used was in the background and partially visible. Jazz zoomed in and enhanced, filling in what was her best guess to tighten and clarify the image. This was tedious work and took time, but she could see the progress on the screen.

Wolf got up to go get snacks from the newly installed fridge. "Want a warm-up?"

"Sure," she muttered as her eyes darted around the screens.

He snagged her cup and topped it off with fresh tea from the R2-D2 pot on the counter. She sipped at it while he handed her a Tastykake Butterscotch Krimpet. She ate it while still typing with one hand. He kept his eyes on the figure as more was brought into focus each time she zoomed in and added more pixels. "I don't recognize that guy at all. Can you do a search for his face on other sites?"

"I'm way ahead of you, sweetheart. Once he's recognizable enough, I'll ping him everywhere I can, starting with local places. Where were the other businesses that got vandalized?"

He told her the addresses, and she was off to the races, looking for other video sources. Several new ones came up.

"That one's different," he noted.

"Security camera from the back of Smitherman's across from Clauson's," Jazz said absently. "It's pointed to the front window and catches a small view of the street. See? There."

The grainy image showed Edna Clauson locking up and not noticing the two figures behind her. One quickly broke out the glass at the door, then lit and lobbed a Molotov cocktail through the opening. The other followed Edna. When she fell to the ground, he pulled down the scarf around his face and spat on her.

"OMG! Did you see that? Disgusting!" Jazz's voice rose. "How can anyone be so nasty and mean?"

Anger was not the word to describe Wolf's gut reaction. Enraged was the closest he could find for the callous disrespect shown to an old woman who, for decades, did nothing more than sell candy and a few staples to the people of this neighborhood. "We got him now. Can you isolate that shot of his face? That asshole is going to pay for what he's done. How's the shooter's image coming?"

"Almost there. Got him as best as he's gonna get. Let's see what turns up regarding his ugly mug." She started the program to zoom and add pixels to the second picture before pinging the restored one.

The computer hummed as it searched. Jazz picked up another Krimpet, then dropped it as she took in the results. "Wolf, do you see this?" She pointed to an image among many she'd pulled from the corners of the web.

His face grew stormy when he saw what she had found. "Fuck."

The second image came more into focus, and before the perpetrator's face became completely clear, Wolf was already on the phone, calling Quillon. "We got a big problem, brother."

24

Zinnia tapped her card on the terminal. "Thanks for taking extra time on my forearms. They've been tight as hell for weeks."

Sabrina smiled as she pulled up her appointment calendar. "No problem. I'm glad I could work you in. Do you want to schedule next month?"

"Can I come in two weeks? I got overtime at the warehouse, and I expect I'll be hurtin' sooner rather than later."

Sabrina winked. "I got you. I have an opening on that Thursday."

Zinnia grinned, showing the large gap between her front teeth. "I'll take it. See you then."

"Very cool."

The burly woman walked out the spa door as

Sabrina rested her elbows on the front counter. Zinnia was one of her favorites. Some clients wanted silence, and Sabrina was okay with that, but it was nice to have open conversations with people. Zinnia liked to ask questions and show genuine interest in what her body needed. The older woman wasn't quite sixty but still worked a very physical job, and it showed in her stressed and tight tendons. Menopause wasn't doing her any favors either. Today she had a hot flash on the table, but both women laughed and joked about the natural process. Clients like Zinnia were a big reason Sabrina loved what she did.

Yeah, she couldn't wait for the next step to put down some real roots in this city. After Cam's big confession, they'd spent the night making love and talking about future plans. Someday, she wanted to run her own massage business. He wanted to set up his own forge. She couldn't wait to see a real snow. He said he'd always wanted to tour the Florida Keys. Because he was still dealing with the cast on his upper arm, she treated him to a blow job before mounting him and—

"What the fuck?"

Instantly, Sabrina's good mood vanished as Cicely stormed into the front foyer. The spa owner pointed an angry finger down the hallway. "Why is there a pile of dirty towels in room four?"

Sabrina took a calming breath before answering. "There's only two of us here for now. I asked you earlier if I could put the used towels in room four until I got a chance to wash them. You said yes."

"I didn't think they would be there all damn day!"

Another calming breath. "Both of us have been going nonstop since we opened. My last client just left, and we're closed for the day. I'll go start a load."

"Laziness is what that is. You could have put something in over your lunch break."

The breaths weren't working. "I did. I'll transfer that load to the dryer and start another wash load."

Cicely's eyes bugged out. "Are you telling me there's a wet load of laundry in there now?"

"Yes, and it just finished cycling about an hour ago. Not long enough to sour, so it should be fine."

"You use too many damn towels and sheets. It's driving my electric up like crazy."

Sabrina reached for more patience and found the well running low. "I can't control how many people walk through those doors, and each of them has to get a clean set of linens and a clean towel."

Cicely rolled her eyes and muttered something

under her breath as she stomped away. Sabrina didn't catch it but decided not to push it. Instead, she focused on her relationship with Cam. Ever since they took it to the next level, it had been one long, sparkly dream. The sex was mind-blowing, but the little moments of intimate connection were better.

Like when he called her to ask if they needed anything from the grocery store.

And took her bike in to fix the V-twin timing.

And cleaned the kitchen after she cooked.

And took out the trash.

And cuddled with her when they watched a Netflix movie.

She knew without a doubt that she loved him. He'd already said he loved her, and he proved it every day by the way he treated her.

Nope, she was not going to let Cicely put a damper on her good mood.

Sabrina calmly walked to the laundry room and switched loads, then returned to the front counter to grab her phone.

"What is this shit?" An iPad clattered next to her as Cicely tossed it onto the glass surface. "Why are all these numbers messed up?"

Sabrina clenched one fist and then forced it to relax as she tamped down on the words she wanted to say. "I don't know. Stephan keeps up with inventory. I expect the counts aren't accurate because he's been at home recuperating."

"More laziness."

The dregs of Sabrina's patience dried up. "Oh. My. God! He was *shot*, for chrissakes! That's got nothing to do with being lazy. What's the matter with you?"

"Nothing's wrong with me except I got a business full of people who are useless."

The sneering tone made Sabrina see red. "Hold on a fucking minute. Stephan getting shot is not some big conspiracy against you."

Cicely threw her hands up in the air, her braids rattling in tandem. "Who the fuck do you think you are? This is *my* business, and these are *my* clients! But they come in and ask for *you* all the fucking time!" She pointed a finger in Sabrina's face. "You *stole* them from me!"

Sabrina's brain short-circuited with incredulity. "You're kidding me, right? You're the one who books people for appointments. I work on the ones *you* send me!"

"And then they book your table again!" She ticked off names on her fingers. "Gayle, Barry, Jeff, Monica, Zinnia—all of them used to come to me, and now they come to you."

Sabrina raised her hand in a shrug. "So what do you want me to do? Give bad massages?"

"I want you to stop stealing my clients!"

"How can I steal clients when they're still coming to your business? Either way, you get paid."

"That's not the point!"

Sabrina had reached her limit. "Well, what *is* your point?"

"The point is—"

Cicely never got to it, as the bell dinged to signal someone had entered the building.

Shit, I forgot to lock the door.

Sabrina swiveled to see who had come in, and her tight face fell. "You've got to be kidding me."

Rodrigo sneered at her, his dark eyes snapping with irritation. "Yeah, good to see you, too, sis." He strode up to the glass counter and slapped a stack of papers next to the iPad. "I'm here. Sign these, and I'll go."

Sabrina's brain overloaded. "I'm not signing anything until I read them."

Rodrigo exploded in a fit of Spanish curses. "I drove up the fucking length of the country to get these damn things signed. Get you a fucking pen and do it."

"Let's try this again," Sabrina started in her saccharine voice. "Well, hello there, Rigo. Nice to see you. I hope you're well. Me? I'm good for the most part." She resumed her angry tone. "Are you deaf, bro? I said I'm not signing until I read what's in those papers. Give me half an hour."

"Bullshit, you'll do it now so I can get back on the fucking road."

She blinked. "It's an eighteen-hour drive."

"Yeah, dumbass, I know. I came up here in one shot to get this shit done 'cause you left me no choice. I gotta have these filed at the courthouse by closing tomorrow or I'm screwed."

Any comprehension Sabrina had left fled. "You won't make it back in time."

"I'll drive fast."

"What about my clients?" Cicely demanded.

"Oh my God!" Sabrina yelled, her attention torn between the two people. "I cannot handle both of you at the same time! Cicely, if you want me to quit, fine! Pay me what you owe me and I'm outta here. Loving Hands Massage has openings, and I'm glad to go talk to them."

Cicely's mouth dropped open. "I don't need you to quit!"

"Then stop this crap about me stealing clients!"

Cicely sniffed and raised her nose in the air before turning away. "You don't have to be so dramatic."

"Seriously?" With a deep breath, Sabrina reined in what she could and faced Rodrigo. "Unless you can teleport or fly, you'll never make it back in time to file tomorrow."

He scoffed. "I wouldn't be in this jam if you'd have come when I called you the first time."

"I'm not a fucking dog, bro. This is not my problem."

"It is when all this fucking paperwork is involved. I got all this shit to sort out with this fuckin' probate mess. Rosa is tryin' to screw me over. Fuckin' old hag!"

Sabrina's head vibrated with an impending headache. She pressed two fingers against her temple. "Is it really that big a deal? How much could there possibly be to inherit?"

"Dad had some money and a whopper life insurance policy. Aunt Rosa is makin' a stink now, sayin' I owe her for convincing Dad to adopt me and for helping raise me. She said without her, I'd have been in a foster home or some shit, so I'd better split my inheritance with her or she'll make my life hell.

She's already talkin' shit to the rest of the family, gettin' them all on her side."

Sabrina's eyes bugged out. "Saint Rosa ain't such a saint now, is she? And how do both of you know I'm not Ernie's daughter by blood?"

Rodrigo sneered. "You don't look like anyone else in the family. Everyone knows that *puta* mother of yours slept around a lot. You could be anyone's kid, like that Scrap guy's."

Sabrina's ire fell away like wilted petals from a plucked daisy. Raquel wanted her to be Scrap's daughter just to inherit and sell his assets. No one wanted her to be Ernie's daughter except for her. And she still had no idea at all about who she came from. It was maddening, and at the same time, depressing.

Rodrigo continued with a dismissive wave of his hand. "None of that shit matters. Your name is still listed as one of the beneficiaries." He picked up the sheaf of papers and shook them at her. "This is saying you relinquish your share 'cause you're not blood kin to him and that you'll turn over your part to me. If I have to, I can just give Rosa some of your half so she'll fuck off."

Then he went there with the coup d'état. "You don't deserve nothing that was *my* dad's."

Heart shot right through the chest. The pain couldn't be any thicker if it was a real bullet. "He was my dad too." Her voice got quiet as she absorbed the verbal blow.

"He was never your dad. You were just a parasite left behind by your mom."

The breath left Sabrina's lungs in a whoosh. Her knees wanted to buckle so badly, and it took every bit of her willpower to stay standing. "That's not true."

Rodrigo opened his mouth to say more when the bell announced someone else.

Specs walked in. His round eyes grew even bigger behind his glasses as he took them in. "Oh, I didn't expect anyone else to be here."

Sabrina didn't know the man very well, only that he had joined the Iron City Knights fairly recently. She remembered he had a cut and a bike and was aces at spreadsheets. That's about it. "I'm sorry, Specs. Did you have a late appointment? We're actually closed."

Cicely came out. "What's going on? Who is this, and why is he here?"

Specs shook his head. "You were supposed to be alone."

That made no sense. Sabrina's gut started churning. Something was wrong. "What are you talking about, Specs?"

The man shrugged. "Guess it doesn't matter."

He pulled out a handgun and fired. The crack made Sabrina jump, her ears ringing with the sudden sound blast. Red bloomed from Rodrigo's stomach, and he fell to the floor.

"Fuck! You shot me, motherfucker!"

Sabrina had no time to react before Specs put a bead on Cicely and another bullet found a spot in her chest.

"What the hell?" Sabrina shrieked as her boss collapsed. "What are you doing?"

Specs turned the gun on her. "Sorry about this."

He reared back his hand.

The last thing Sabrina remembered was the arc of the gun just before it slammed into her temple.

25

Cam looked at his phone again. He'd texted Sabrina to tell her he'd be late coming home as Wolf had an important update for the club. She should have left the spa by now, and he was surprised she hadn't responded yet. Normally, she checked in when she left to go home to see if he needed anything she could pick up on the way. So far, nothing, but he didn't want to put any alarms out quite yet. Maybe her phone died or she had bad reception. There were a few dead spots between the spa and the house.

The house. Home. *Their* home. Sabrina was sticking with him. He felt like he'd won the lottery. He wished Vera and Cecil were still alive to see this.

"Anyone know where Specs is?" Wolf asked. His

face was long, grim, and full of menace. Something had enraged the club president, and whatever or whoever started it might die tonight.

Only Quillon dared to speak. "Specs? He said he had some family business to take care of tonight. Why?"

"Look at this." Wolf opened a laptop and spun it around so everyone could see the screen. "Jazz worked her magic on these videos. See for yourselves."

The rest of the Knights stayed silent as they stared at the moving figures. They'd already seen the first video once: two men vandalizing the coffee shop. The part they didn't see the first time was the reflection of the front window. Jazz had enhanced the picture, and a clear face showed up.

It looked a lot like Specs.

"What the fuck is this?" Melter asked as rumblings started around the table.

"Keep watching," Wolf ordered.

The next video took place outside Clauson's. The shot angle came from above the front of the store. It showed Edna locking up and walking away just as two men came around from the other side of the corner store. One man broke the glass while another lit a Molotov and threw it into the opening. The frame froze and zoomed in on one of them. The man's face was obscured behind a mask, but the open neck of his hoodie revealed a chain with a silver skull dangling from it.

The same one Specs usually wore.

"Son of a bitch," someone muttered.

The next video started, this time outside Hob's place. The group watching collectively inhaled as they saw Garfield enter his shop. Two men went in a few minutes later. The next cut came from another reflection that looked like a dashcam from someone's car. A wave of anger rolled off the Knights as they watched the brutal beating.

White-hot rage filled Cam as scene after scene came up. Each one showed a piece of something that led back to Specs. Yet it wasn't the Specs they knew. This guy moved with confidence and calculation, not the nerdy shuffling of someone trying to please everyone.

If Specs wasn't Specs, who the hell was this man?

Wolf's condemnation rang colder than ice. "Specs betrayed this club. He's been behind all these attacks throughout the area this whole time. We don't know who his partner is, but I want some fucking answers, and I want them now. Who vetted him for membership?"

The Knights glanced at one another in confusion.

"Do you mean to tell me no one checked this guy out before admitting him?"

Ratchet answered for the club. "We thought you did."

Wolf raised his eyes to the ceiling and cursed. "Does anyone know where he lives?"

Again, the Knights had no answers.

"How the fuck are we supposed to find him, then?"

Melter, of all people, spoke up. "The partner got shot, right? At the rally?"

"Yeah."

Melter cleared his throat. "I'm guessing he wouldn't go to any hospitals 'cause they have to report any GSWs and everyone is on high alert from the shooting, right? Well, my... friend... told me he's had an uptick in... pharma sales lately. Some guy asking for fennies or oxys or morph."

"So?"

"Same guy also wanted antibiotics. The ones you can't get without a prescription."

Wolf lost any patience he had left. "Melter, make your fucking point."

"He said it was a Knight who wanted 'em. He

said the guy bought a bunch of stuff from him and then scrammed like his ass was on fire. I wondered who might have a drug problem and why they needed antibiotics too."

"Why didn't you say anything earlier?"

Melter shrugged. "It's not my business if someone wants to get high now and then. Now I'm thinking that might be our guy, ya know?"

Frustrated moans sounded around the table, and Wolf clenched his fists as he raised them. Explosion appeared imminent, but he visibly pulled back from the brink. "What does that have to do with Specs and the shooting?"

Again, Melter shrugged. "Denny checked for gunshot wounds at the hospitals n'at, right? Maybe they're treating it themselves. Painkillers and antibiotics."

Quillon spoke up before Wolf could go off. "It's a possibility. If that's what's happening, then it makes sense to get that shit close to where you're hiding. Where does your dealer operate?"

Melter hesitated before confessing, "He's around the strip district."

The strip district had begun as an industrial area of foundries and mills. As time moved on, so did those businesses. A recent revival brought the area back into favor as a big shopping place with a bunch of different specialty shops and a variety of restaurants. It was a big tourist attraction, so why a drug dealer chose that spot for his trade made little sense, but these days, very little did.

"What are the chances someone can identify a rogue Knight? We're not very popular over there," Crossman said.

Wolf stood up. "Let's go see. Colors on. We ride in formation as a show of force. People will try to avoid us, but the shopkeepers will talk to get us to leave. Someone has to know something. Melter, you find your connection and see if he has any more information."

Melter shook his head. "He's not gonna like me throwing him under the bus."

"I don't give a shit. We need to find this motherfucker now."

Quillon nodded in agreement and tapped his fingers in a rolling rhythm on the tabletop. "So, do we tell Denny about this?"

Wolf's face grew hard. Currently, a lot of friction existed between the leader of the Knights and the police officer. "Not yet. The law is the law, and justice is justice. Sometimes they don't agree." His phone buzzed. The man snorted when he saw the caller.

"Speak of the devil." He flicked the screen with his thumb and put the device to his ear. "Yeah?"

Darkness clouded his face, putting everyone on high alert. "Where are they now?" He listened for a moment, then hung up without saying goodbye. His eyes went straight to Cam. "You need to stay cool."

Worse words had never been spoken.

As Wolf informed the group about the latest shooting, everyone's attention shifted to Cam. Gunshots reported at Sunstone Healing. Two victims on the way to the hospital. A witness stated they'd seen a Knight loading an unconscious woman into a car and driving away. Blonde.

A fury like nothing he'd ever experienced erupted in Cam's gut. Stay cool? Yeah, right. He'd stay as cool as an ice cube in the Sahara. "I'm going to kill him."

Wolf nodded once. "We gotta find him first. Let's ride."

26

Sabrina wasn't sure what woke her up, the sounds or the smell. One voice cursed like crazy and another moaned in pain. Both were angry. She could make out some words, but not enough to form coherent sentences. The stench was awful, like sour piss and ass covered in Pine-Sol. The combination was gag worthy, and she hoped she wouldn't vomit.

Gag was right, as there was something across her mouth and she couldn't spit it out. She tried to lift her hand to her face, but it wouldn't move. *Fuck, I'm tied down!* She became more aware of that fact as she pulled her limbs to test the strength and range of her bonds. Her arms and legs were helpless, spread-eagle across the firmest mattress she'd ever lain on.

Be still and think! She forced her breathing and heart rate to slow, deliberately taking in deeper air despite the stink, holding and letting it out in equal measure. The two people's voices became clearer. Men. Angry and cursing. One sounded familiar, and the other sounded hurt.

"If you'd stop eating them like candy, maybe they'd last longer."

"You try getting shot and dealing with this kind of pain."

"You were supposed to stay hidden."

"How could I do that in an open park? That was your idea, ya stupid jagoff!"

For a moment, nothing made sense, but then her heart jumped into her throat.

Park? Getting shot? These two were involved with the rally shooting! And if that was the case, they might also be the ones who had been terrorizing the neighborhood with the vandalism.

Clarity made her heart jump again.

Omigod! Rodrigo! Cicely!

She didn't have time to wonder if someone had gotten them to the hospital. A splash of cold water landed on her face, and she choked on it as it went up her nose. For a moment, she couldn't breathe.

Then the gag was ripped away from her mouth and she gasped for air.

"I thought you were awake. Welcome back, bitch."

Her sinuses burned from the dousing, and she continued to cough and retch. The man who stood above her looked like Specs, but not the one who'd been in charge at the rally, running around with a clipboard full of spreadsheets in one hand and multiple pens in the other. This man was cold. Calculating. And angry. Very, very angry.

"Specs," she murmured, and a cruel smile appeared on the man's face.

"So you do recognize me." He gave a sardonic grunt.

"Who are you really?"

He sneered at her. "No one you'd know. Those dumbass bikers don't have a fucking clue who I am either."

Adrenaline flooded her body, and keeping still became harder. Her concentration was split between listening to Specs 2.0 and fighting the urge to twist against her bonds. "I just remember your name and that you're good with organization. Otherwise, they're not the only ones who don't have a clue."

His smile widened, and icy fingers trailed down her spine. "I can't blame you. This is shit that happened before your time."

A faint trembling in her belly threatened to explode. *Keep it together, Sabrina!* "Care to share? I'm rather curious about why I'm here."

A groan from the other side of the room interrupted their conversation. "For fuck's sake, I need another pill!"

Specs rolled his eyes. "My brother." He leaned in close, as if to impart a secret, and Sabrina cringed away. "Don't go anywhere."

She craned her neck to see where Specs moved. She had a sliver of vision to see another man lying across the corner of a small couch that had seen better days. He was on his back with a large pad of towels around his middle. What did that mean for bullets? Were they still inside him? "He needs a hospital."

"Fuck that. The shot grazed through his side. He's not pissing blood, so's nothing major was hit. All he needs is painkillers and antibiotics. We're not taking any chances that the Knights will find us. Not 'til we're through."

"Through with what?"

"Taking vengeance."

The man on the couch coughed and yelled in pain. "Goddammit, I need another fucking pill!"

Specs muttered and rolled his eyes. "Hold your horses." He picked up a plastic baggie with a rainbow of tablets, selected a few, and handed them to the writhing man. "You need to lay off these for a while or else you're gonna run out. These were hard as hell to score."

Sabrina strained her eyes as she watched the man pop the pills into his mouth and chew them with sharp, crunching movements. *Ugh! I bet that tastes awful!* "What did the Knights do to you that you have to take vengeance?"

Specs handed his brother a bottle of water. "Not just the Knights. They're the ones at the top of the chain, and we're building up to them. No, it's revenge for our sister."

Sister? Sabrina clenched her fists as her body started twitching from her on-edge nerves. "I don't understand."

Specs strode back over to the bed. "I think you probably should have a better picture to get why this is happening to you." He pulled a pocketknife from the back of his jeans and flicked it open. Sabrina's heart pounded, fear sweat breaking out across her body.

"Our sister used to dance at Attic, under the name Candy Sweet. She used to beat me and Billy up regularly when we were growing up. Gave our parents such grief that when she left the house at eighteen, they were ready for her to get out. A real piece of work. I'm surprised she never got pregnant in high school."

Sabrina didn't know how to respond. What did one say to a brother talking about his sister in such a negative way? Especially when he just said he practically hated her growing up.

Specs tested the blade against his thumb. "We heard from her a few times over the years, but mostly to tell us when people fucked with her. About how those two gay coffee shop owners barred her from their place and how the local corner store banned her."

He huffed a laugh. "The bookstore owner asked her to leave and not come back. The shoe repair guy was the worst. He fixed her heels a few times and she always paid him, but the one time she didn't have money, he refused, even after she offered a blow job instead."

The man on the couch moaned, and Specs snarled at him. "Shut the fuck up, Billy. I'm sick of hearing your fucking whining."

"Fuck you!"

No lost love between these two, Sabrina thought as Specs picked up an ashtray and chucked it at his brother. The glass hit its mark, and Billy cried out in pain.

"The truth is, Candy brought shit on herself. She'd be the one to start fights between her boyfriends at school and laugh it up when they beat each other to a pulp," Specs continued. "I bet she mouthed off one too many times at the coffee shop and shoplifted regularly at the corner store. I don't know about the book place, but I'm not surprised about the shoe repair guy. I'd rather have the money, too, instead of getting sucked off."

He stopped playing with his knife and looked Sabrina directly in the eye. "Candy was a slut and a bitch who cared nothing for no one. She used people as long as she benefitted from it, and when she no longer did, she'd cut them loose with no remorse."

"What does that have to do with the spa? What did Cicely do to her?"

Specs grinned evilly. "Nothing. We just needed you."

The trembling got worse, and she tightened every muscle she had, pulling at the bonds holding her down. Even though it was futile, she gave in to the need to fight. "Why? What does any of this have to do with me?"

In one motion, Specs grabbed the top of her shirt and jammed the knife through it, ripping it open from top to bottom. Sabrina let out a startled scream as the tip of the blade grazed her stomach. Specs brushed his fingers over her opened skin.

"She was still my sister. My beautiful, fucked-up Candy Sweet, and I loved her so much." His voice cracked as he began to cry.

Sabrina's instincts picked up on his crazy tone. Shit just got weirder and weirder.

Specs wiped his eyes, leaving behind two streaks of red across his face. It was blood. *Her* blood. "The Knights fired her from the strip club. She loved dancing there so much, and they booted her out like she was trash. Then she was murdered right here in this motel. In this room."

The waterworks immediately stopped, and his face turned vicious. "You know all about fucked-up family shit. Is it any real surprise we want revenge?"

Sabrina's skin burned where the blade made contact. Specs peeled back the ruined shirt and slipped the blade between her breasts to slice open her bra. The cups parted, exposing her breasts to the air. There was nothing she could do about it. Specs pinched one nipple and then the other, twisting them painfully and making her cry out.

"You're a Knight's woman. You're gonna die like Candy did. I'm gonna fuck you while I cut you up and then strangle you to death as I come."

27

Cam's heavy footfalls rang through the waiting room. Fifteen steps one way and fifteen steps back. Cicely and the man were in surgery. It didn't look good for either of them.

After Wolf gave everyone the news that Sabrina was missing, Cam went a little nuts. Panic circled his brain along with the urge to go find her. But he had no place to start. Specs? He assumed that's who had her, but no way to confirm. Where? Jazz hacked into CCTV footage around the spa, but the feeds were spotty.

He'd rushed to Sunstone, but Denny ran him off.

"Camshaft, I get that you're worried, but you're in my way. Go to the hospital and wait there. I promise I'll call you directly when we know more."

An officer took pictures of a big pile of papers on the floor. Denny picked them up and read through a few before thrusting them at Cam. "Know anything about this?"

A few quick sentences told Cam this had to do with Ernie's estate. He saw the words distribution *and* relinquish *before handing them back. "No, but it looks like part of her dad's estate paperwork. Right now I don't give a shit. We need to find Sabrina."*

Fifteen steps. Turn. Check phone for texts.

Nothing.

It was driving him crazy. He wanted to run the streets to look for her, shouting her name and tearing apart the city brick by brick until he found her. Wolf ordered him to stand down.

"You still got a bum arm, brother. I get that it's killin' you, but you need to let us do this part. We'll find her. I'll get Jazz on this pronto. Until we get a hit, you need to stay put and stay cold. Screaming at the moon won't do jack shit for your woman."

The man with bullets in his gut was probably Rodrigo. So far, no one had identified the guy to him, but based on what Sabrina told him and the paperwork Denny showed him, he figured it was a good guess. He must have gotten tired of waiting and come up here to force Sabrina to deal with the probate mess. Bad timing on his part.

Fifteen steps. Turn.

If what he'd caught with his quick glance at the paperwork was correct, Sabrina might have some money coming to her after all. Not a never-work-again fortune, but a nice-sized chunk that would help her get on her feet and give her some breathing room. He'd bet his left nut that Rodrigo wanted her to sign away her rights to that inheritance.

What a dick.

A dick who could be dying right now.

Fuck.

Fifteen steps. Check phone for texts.

A thought hit him hard.

Scrap. Did anyone think to contact him?

Cam didn't have Scrap's number, but he had Baghouse's. He paused in his pacing and scrolled to that name. "Yo, Baghouse, did anyone talk to Scrap yet?"

"I'm with him now. He's not doing too good."

In the background, Cam heard Scrap's gravelly bellow. "Who the hell is that? What about my daughter?"

Baghouse yelled back, "Shut the fuck up, ya

jagoff! I can't hear anything, and you still don't know if she *is* your kid!"

Cam paced fourteen steps this time. He must have miscounted or his strides got longer.

Baghouse got back on the line. "He's out of his fuckin' mind. What do we know?"

Cam breathed through his nose. "Nothing much. Waiting for Jazz to find something. Denny's at the spa last I heard. Cicely and Rodrigo are still in surgery. I'm walking a fucking groove into this floor."

"Who the hell is Rodrigo?"

"Sabrina's stepbrother." Fifteen steps. "I don't know how to contact Raquel."

"Don't bother. That bitch will turn up eventually if there's money to be had. She's like a spider, just waiting for a strand of her web to jiggle."

Sixteen steps this time.

"What the fuck is happening?" Scrap shouted in the background.

Cam paused his pacing once more. He had no answers. Helplessness lodged deep in his gut, and he was ready to start screaming himself. The need to punch something hard until it broke into smaller and smaller pieces rose inside him. Right now he could hammer raw, cold steel and it wouldn't faze him.

Sabrina, where are you?

His phone buzzed, and Wolf's name appeared. Cam's heart started racing. "Hold on, Wolf's calling." Before Baghouse said anything, Cam switched over. "Yeah?"

"Jazz got a hit. You're not gonna believe this."

The pounding organ in his chest leaped to his throat when Wolf told him the location. He was on the other side of town. "If he's hurt her…."

"I got it, brother. We're almost there. Just so you know, we're not waiting for you, so get your ass here pronto."

Cam hung up and ran from the waiting room.

28

"You son of a bitch! Fucking asshole!"

Sabrina fought the bonds, cussing and screaming as Specs methodically cut the clothes from her body. No way would she make it easier for him to rape her. Her movements meant that the knife occasionally made contact with her skin, leaving red streaks behind.

"Cocksucker!"

He backhanded her across her face, and she saw stars as her head whipped to the side.

"Shut the fuck up, bitch!"

She spat blood out. "You get your jollies from abusing women? Is that how you get off?"

"I said shut up!" Foam splattered from his mouth, hitting her cheeks.

Ugh, gross! "No!"

"Just cut her throat and be done with it," Billy groaned from the couch. "I need another pill."

"I just gave you one," Specs snapped at him. "That was the last of them."

"I need it!"

"Fuck off!" Specs picked up something else and threw it at his brother. Sabrina couldn't tell what it was, but apparently it hurt, as Billy yelped.

She stilled for a moment as the two men squabbled. The longer they argued and the longer she held out, perhaps there was a chance Cam or one of the Knights would find her before *it* happened. She'd screamed about how she was being raped, but in a place like this, no one paid any attention. Maybe she should start yelling "fire" or "police" or something more meaningful. When she opened her mouth to shout again, he punched her in the face several times.

"Do you ever listen? Shut. The. Fuck. *Up!*"

Her nose broke with a crunch, and her vision blurred with the strikes. Damn, that one hurt. Breathing became harder to do as blood trickled down her throat and her eyes started to swell. No doubt the mortician would have to work some fancy makeup magic to make her presentable for the funeral.

She could barely make out Specs's fuzzy image as he lowered his jeans and grabbed his dick, trying to rub it to life.

"Can't ged id up, you fuckin' loser?" If she was going to die, she'd fight like hell until the end.

"How the hell does Cam put up with you?" the small man growled as he pulled at the limp little sausage.

"He'z a man. A real man."

That was the last straw for Specs. He picked up his belt and whipped her across her belly and thighs. "Goddamn cunt! Don't know when to keep your fucking mouth shut!"

Sabrina screamed in pain. Welts appeared with each blow. More work for the mortician, she reasoned.

Finally, the beating stopped as Specs ran out of steam. He straddled her body, and she tried weakly to toss him off. He looped the belt around her throat and slowly tightened it, cutting off her airway.

Whatever fight she had left in her disappeared fast. Her arms and legs twitched uselessly as he choked her, the leather cutting into her skin as he pulled harder and harder. Her eyeballs felt like they were about to burst from her skull, and her pulse pounded in her ears.

This is it. I'm done. Cam, I love you. I wish I'd told you more often. Heal and move on, baby.

The belt suddenly relaxed and the weight on top of her eased as Specs climbed off her and scuttled to the door, jerking his pants up as he moved. She gasped for what air she could as he pressed his ear against the wood.

"What's happening?" Billy questioned.

"I don't—"

He suddenly fell back as someone forced the door open and a figure that looked a lot like Wolf filled the frame. A furious Wolf.

Sabrina lost her limited sight of the two men and had a hard time making out what the sounds were, but if she guessed right, Specs was getting the shit beaten out of him. Stalemate's form came to her side and cut through the ropes that held her.

"Shit. Cam's gonna freakin' go off."

"Get her out of here."

"Where's Cam?"

"On the way."

Various voices surrounded her as her arms and legs were released. The stretching of her joints for so long made it hard for her to move them. Stalemate slipped an arm under her knees and head to lift her when she heard Cam shouting for her.

"Sabrina! Fuck, can you hear me, baby?"

"Ayah," she croaked.

His face appeared in front of hers. Even with her bad eyes, she could see him. He looked wonderful.

"Hospital. Now." That one sounded like Wolf.

"Was she raped?"

"Don't think so."

Sabrina tried to swallow and then rasped, "He didn't make it. Couldn't get his mini-wiener hard."

A wave of heat blew from Cam, intense enough that she felt it over her entire body.

"If I have my way, he won't have to worry about ever getting hard again."

Wolf intervened. "I know you want blood, but trust me and get your woman to the ER, brother. I promise we got this."

"Wolf," Cam gritted out, the word carrying rivers of fury and mountains of frustration.

Sabrina sensed his need for vengeance as a tangible emotion. She coughed and made another effort to speak and be understood. "Cam, I think I need a doctor."

"Fuck!" exploded from Cam's mouth. "You let those motherfuckers know this isn't over."

The leader of the Knights inclined his head. "You have my word."

Cam moved to lift her, but Crossman got there first. "Let me. You'll fuck up your arm again."

"You're killin' me, man."

Crossman inclined his head. "I know, but I'm also protecting you."

Sabrina held her breath against the pain as she was lifted and cradled against the biker's chest. If her eyes had worked better, she would have seen Specs and Billy trussed up on the floor. She sought Cam's hazy figure as an adrenaline crash got closer.

"Love you," she grated out. "Just wanted you to remember that."

"Love you, too, babe."

AFTER CAM AND CROSSMAN MADE THEIR WAY OUTSIDE to the waiting car, Stalemate regarded Specs and his brother lying on the floor. Both men were bound with zip ties and gags and sported bloody, bruised faces. "Do we call Denny or clean this up ourselves?"

Wolf faced the younger man, and a silent message passed between them. The Iron City Knights' president had ice-cold murder in his eyes.

He could kill the two men and not be bothered at all. He raised an eyebrow as if asking a question.

The large man shrugged and clicked his teeth. "I can get rid of the bodies with no traces left to find."

Wolf nodded. "I promised Cam his time. He's gotta take care of his woman now. And we're gonna take care of him."

29

"We got a tip call. Don't know who," Ratchet told Denny.

Cam heard them talking outside the emergency room doors. He stood just beyond the curtains as several nurses worked on Sabrina. He didn't want her out of his sight, but he would have to deal with the police at some point.

The officer showed up at the hospital after Wolf called him to say they'd found Sabrina. Someone informed him that she'd been beaten and strangled, but there were no signs of her attackers.

"They must have heard we were coming and bolted," Ratchet continued with a shrug. "Who knows what morons like that are thinking?"

"Yeah, who knows if they're gonna be bothering

folks again?" Cam had no trouble hearing the skepticism in Denny's voice.

Ratchet sighed with practiced overexaggeration. "I hope not."

Cam came out of the emergency bay area. "What do you want, Officer?"

His bitter tone asked more than the words. The underlying question was *"Are you here as a policeman or as a friend?"*

Denny straightened his spine. "I need to talk to Sabrina when she's stable."

"Kinda hard for her to do that since that animal nearly choked her to death. They're stitching her up now. Some of those cuts went deep."

"You sure it was Specs?"

"Yes."

The one-word answer preceded a stare-off between the officer and the Knight. Neither of them moved an inch.

Denny was the first one to break. "You know where he is?"

"Not a clue." Cam gave a quick, jerky shake of his head. Inside it, he finished his thought. *But I know where he's going.*

"Don't do anything stupid, son."

Rage nearly consumed Cam's vision. He pointed

at the floor. "You see me sitting here? Waiting for my woman? The one that goddamn piece of shit attacked and almost killed, remember? Where else would I be, ya jagoff?" He held up his arm and knocked on the cast. "Don't forget about this shit."

Denny's mouth hardened at the jagoff insult, but he said nothing. "You know the drill. You hear anything, you let me know ASAP, yeah?"

"That fucker has a lot of enemies now, Officer. Not just me and not just the Knights. He and his brother hurt a lot of people. Killed more than one. There are plenty out there who would love to see him gone and not think twice about doing a soft-shoe dance on his grave."

"I get it. But I'm also an officer of the law and I swore an oath, much as it pains me sometimes."

Cam relaxed a little. "Respect."

Denny heaved a long sigh. "I guess I'm done here for now. Call me when she's able to answer questions, yeah?"

"That will be up to her."

There was nothing else Denny could say or do. He left the waiting room and headed toward the parking deck.

The doors swished open, and a young female doctor appeared. "She's stable, and her vitals are all good. Breathing on her own, although it hurts like hell. She'll be sore for a few days. I'm sending her home with some painkillers and muscle relaxers. Lots of rest."

The doctor shifted her glasses from her nose to rest on her head, effectively pulling back her mane of black hair. "You've seen her. She's got a significant amount of bruising and swelling around her face and eyes. There's some petechia in the whites, so you'll see some redness where a few capillaries burst. We don't think her vision is compromised, but it's a good idea to follow up with an ophthalmologist."

With every word the pretty doctor spoke, Cam's fury ratcheted up. He wanted to call Wolf with a location, but his president had told him to stay put.

"That's your alibi, and it's rock solid. She needs you more than you need to be with us. We're gonna take care of it, yeah?"

The need to kill something was almost unbearable, especially when he went back to the curtained alcove where Sabrina lay in pristine white sheets. Her eyes were covered with compresses, but the dark purple was still visible.

He'd seen the cuts.

He'd seen the bruises.

He'd seen the blood.

Rage like he'd never experienced ignited in his gut, and he visualized taking his favorite knife and slowly carving pieces off the man who did this to his woman. He'd start with fingers, then the nose, ears, lips, working his way down to his balls and dick. He'd leave the eyes for last so that fucker could see everything.

"Cam? Is that you?"

Sabrina's weak voice brought him back. He gasped for air when he realized he'd stopped breathing while he fantasized about the torture he'd inflict. "I'm right here, baby." He moved forward and took her hand, the one that didn't have an IV in it. "Right here."

"Can you get me an ice cream cone? Like that butterscotch one from the rally."

Tears filled his eyes at the request. "Sure thing, sweetheart."

"Good. I'm gonna need the energy to kick some ass."

30

Stalemate scattered another bag of kitty litter on the ground just in case there was any blood or vomit or other expelled fluids. Easy to remove from the concrete floor and dump in the river. Apply a coat of muriatic acid and any traces would be gone. The row of abandoned garages sat behind more long, empty warehouses close to the river. He'd taken care to cover the place with black tarps so no light shone through, but this isolated area seldom saw any kind of traffic. Not even horny teenagers had discovered this spot yet. Still, it was best to take precautions.

Can't be too safe. He chuckled at the thought.

The metal building had no insulation and radiated the cold weather, but he had a feeling they wouldn't be here long.

Wolf stood on one side. Cam wanted to be here to get his strip of flesh, but Wolf convinced him his place was with his woman. Stalemate didn't blame Cam for his desire to beat the ever-loving shit out of these two scum-suckers, but the airtight alibi was more important. This club was slowly being built on trust, a most precious commodity. He admired that.

Scrap and Baghouse were present and the only ones seated. Quillon and Crossman manned the strip club, providing other alibis to anyone who asked. Stalemate hadn't seen a lot of Scrap, but he'd heard about him. The old man might appear frail with failing health, but the expression on his face would make the fiercest soldier cower in fear.

Stalemate hoped to have a chess game or two with the former president.

Specs and his brother were tied down and stretched out on rough plank tables. Once they were done here, those pieces of wood could be easily cut up and used as kindling in the outdoor fireplace at Cam's house.

Stalemate started thinking the Knights were due for a family barbecue. He grinned as he picked up a thick towel with a popular chain hotel's logo on it. He walked over to where Specs lay and wrapped it over the man's face, effectively muffling the cursing and screaming. Stalemate looked at Wolf. "You want the first one?"

Wolf showed no emotion as he picked up two large pitchers of ice-cold water and started pouring them onto the towel one after the other. For almost a minute, the sound of splashing water and the creak of the plank table as Specs struggled against his bonds filled the air.

Stalemate released the cloth, and Specs gagged, coughed, and choked as he fought to drag air into his lungs.

Billy looked on, the whites of his eyes showing in pure terror. "Why are you doing this?"

Stalemate shrugged. "We need some answers. There were some rumors out there about the old Slaggers MC colors bein' seen around town. Personally? I think it was a bullshit stunt to throw us off, but we still need to check. Who are you working for?"

"No one!" Billy shouted in desperation.

"You sure about that?"

"Yes! Yes!"

"I believe you, but that fella over there?" He

pointed to Scrap. "He's not so sure. So let's try this again."

Stalemate headed over to Billy's plank, and the man started crying with hysterical sobs. The biker paused and cocked his head to the side. "Now that's a surprise. I thought you were the big tough guy. The one who shot up a rally from a bad sniper position. Surely any man who can shoot at a kid can take a little water up the nose. We dealt with a lot worse in Iraq."

The sharp smell of urine emanated from Billy as he pissed himself. "Please, please, please... I'm sorry... I'm—"

Scrap lost patience. "Can we get this shit done before I die?"

Stalemate draped the soaked towel over Billy's face as Wolf refilled the pitchers.

Billy fought weakly for a while, then lay still. Stalemate whipped the towel off the man and slapped him back to consciousness. "Not yet, tough guy. We still have questions."

Billy came back much like Specs, heaving and choking.

Wolf stood between the two at their heads. He held the pitchers loosely in either hand. "Which one of you kicked the old lady? Edna."

Billy garbled out, "He did!"

"What about Garfield Hob? Who beat him up?"

"He did! He did it all!"

Specs found his voice. "Shut up!"

The whole story came out amid gasps and coughs. Candy Sweet. The family history. Specs's obsession with their sister. His need for revenge. The plans they made and how they were executed. Specs calling the cops after they attacked Hob to throw any suspicion off them.

"He had this thing for Candy, and when she got killed, he lost it."

"Shut the fuck up, Billy!"

The more Billy spilled, the darker Wolf went. Stalemate saw him go completely black before it was over.

"So, no association with a group called the Slaggers?" Wolf asked.

"No gangs. Just us," Billy said.

Stalemate gave a satisfied nod. "Good to know, but just in case someone is lying...."

The cloth came down over the screaming man's mouth and nose.

Wolf filled the pitchers again. "We've got about five gallons left."

"Might as well use it up."

31

Sabrina stared at the letter in Scrap's hand. She noticed a fine shake to the innocent envelope. Plain white, printed address, canceled stamp from the post office—it appeared like any other piece of mail.

However, whatever was in this letter had the power to change both their lives irreversibly.

She'd spent the last two weeks recovering from the kidnapping and torture at the hands of the Sweet brothers. The bruising around her throat had almost faded completely, and her voice finally lost its hoarseness. The cuts were well on the way to healing and would fade with time.

Cam received a text while sitting by her bedside that first night. One word.

> Wolf: Done.

She didn't want to confirm what that meant, but she felt Specs and Billy would not be coming back. Cam stayed with her during her talk with Denny, holding her hand the entire time. She felt each of his reactions as she recounted her story. The flinches, jerks, and tightening told her he heard every word.

Sabrina's own palms were sweating as she sat in Scrap's pitiful little house. She'd insisted this morning that she could do this on her own and didn't need Cam to be there. Holy shit, that was a mistake. Her heart pounded so hard she imagined her body jerking with each beat. Yeah, she could have used Cam's steadiness right about now.

Scrap coughed and smacked his dry lips. "You sure you want to know?"

No, I'm not sure. I'm not sure at all.

"Do you want me to open it?" she asked.

Scrap's hand shook more. "I can do it. Just give me a minute."

The clock on the wall ticked away one minute. Then another. Then another.

"The light's not gonna get any greener." Sabrina sighed. "Treat it like a Band-Aid and just rip it off."

Scrap let out a grunt, then in one movement tore

open the envelope and pulled out the single paper inside. He flicked it open as he put a pair of readers on his face. His eyes squinted anyway, his eyebrows furrowed in concentration.

Sabrina stared at his face with intent as he read the letter. His lips thinned and pressed together. He dropped the paper to his lap. A moment later, he tore off the glasses and pressed the heel of his hand to his single eye.

"What does it say?" Sabrina held her breath. White noise filled her ears as she waited for whatever fate decided.

"You're not my daughter."

Her heart jumped in her chest. Conflicting emotions flooded her mind. Relief. Sorrow. Happiness. Regret. They circled in a war with one another until she was filled with confusion about what to think or feel. The news was both wanted and unwanted, and she had no words to say that seemed to fit.

Scrap appeared to be in the same state. He showed the paper to her, and she read the words herself.

Neither of them spoke for several moments.

Scrap refolded the letter and tucked it back into the envelope. He cleared his throat and coughed a few more times. "Well, I guess that's it."

Sabrina swallowed hard against the lump that suddenly formed. "Yeah, I guess so."

"You okay?"

She could have lied and told him she was peachy as hell, but she had more respect for this man than that. "Honestly, no. No, I'm not okay. I still don't know for sure if Ernie was my dad or not. Hell, from what I've learned, it could be some random guy Mom picked up at a truck stop when she made her way from Pennsylvania to Florida." Her sinuses grew heavy with unshed tears. "I guess I'll never really know, and I'll have to accept that."

Scrap sniffed and flicked a finger at his eye. "Sorry."

Sabrina laughed as tears dripped down her face. "Not your fault." She sat up straight and wiped her cheeks with the back of her hand. "I'm a grown-ass woman. I have a successful career I love and can stand on my own two feet. I have a man who loves me and a badass biker family who accept me. There's plenty of people who have it a lot worse than I do."

"You got bigger balls than a lotta men I know," Scrap told her as he set the letter on the side table.

"For what it's worth, if I did have a daughter, I would hope she'd be just like you."

She felt that compliment deep in her soul. He might not share her DNA after all, but he sat solidly in her corner. That in itself was a great achievement. "Thank you."

Scrap waved a dismissive hand in the air. "Go get that chess board and let's have a game. Doesn't matter who you are, I'll still whip your ass."

Sabrina laughed. "You'll try."

EPILOGUE

Denny entered Attic in his civilian clothes. His general attitude was that when he had on his uniform, he was on duty. After work was a different story; he could just be himself.

At least that was his intent tonight. Whatever he heard in conversation would stay right here with all the other secrets he suspected the Knights had under their belts.

One of the girls danced with full enthusiasm on the stage. Fake tits, fake hair, and fake tan, but genuine moves. She'd had some training at one time in her life. Melter, Ratchet, Stalemate, and Crossman sat at the Knights' normal spot at the round tables off in one corner. Their conversation carried over the music.

"Didja bang your Date Knight girl?" Ratchet took a big swallow of beer, spilling some over his chin.

Melter's eyes bugged out. "No, dude, and get this: The woman won't stop calling me!"

"You should totally bang her." Ratchet suddenly raised an eyebrow. "Wait, did you just call me *dude*?"

"Yeah?"

"You high?"

Melter's lopsided grin gave it away. "Yeah, I am."

Stalemate took a drink of his beer. "Did you bang yours? Even though she outweighed you by a hundred pounds or more?"

Ratchet placed two fingers over his mouth and waggled his tongue between them. "What do you think?"

"Seriously, Ratch, I hope you showed her some respect on the date," Crossman groused.

Ratchet laughed. "You, my friend, got the cream of the crop. What's her name, the girl from the bookstore? Hot, my friend. Banging hot."

Denny moved on through the club to find the president.

Wolf stood at his normal sentry post and jutted his chin at him. "Officer."

Denny expected the cold greeting. For the last couple of weeks, he and the club had been at odds over the disappearance of the Sweet brothers. Then the investigation ended and the whole event became nothing more than a brief blip in the news cycle. Journalists had already moved on to the next story and the next crisis.

"Wolf. I'm just Denny tonight. Long day filling out a shit ton of paperwork and forms. The Sweet brothers are on their way to the crematorium. We found a distant cousin who'd vaguely heard of them. Once he found out there was no money, he signed off, and the state is paying to have them taken care of."

Wolf let out an exaggerated sigh. "Too bad."

Denny played along. "Not really. The system is so backed up it would have been years before they'd gone to trial. Feeding and housing them, costing the taxpayers money. Then people gotta deal with jury duty. It's a pain in the ass, especially when everyone knows the outcome. Nah, it's not a bad thing for those two to drown while making a run out of state on the river. Good thing those bodies washed up and we could make a positive ID. Seems they got pretty banged up on shore rocks. If we hadn't, we'd still be investigating."

Wolf nodded in agreement but stayed silent as the officer kept talking.

"Saves a lot of headaches. Paperwork is finished and filed. As far as I'm concerned, this case is over and done with, and we can all move on to better shit."

Wolf's face remained impassive. "Good to know. First beer is on the house."

THE PHONE ON THE TABLE BUZZED IMPATIENTLY. CAM paused with the lifted hammer in his hand. His arm ached from nonuse all these weeks, but getting back to work in the forge felt good. Real good.

However, a break wouldn't be a bad idea. That and some care from his personal in-house massage therapist.

Cam grinned big as he picked up the phone and glanced at the number. Then his face fell as he saw it was Kyle who was calling. He took a breath and swiped to answer. "Yo, what's up?"

"Tammie left the rehab last week and was found this morning in Nashville. Overdose. She's gone."

A stab of pain hit Cam's heart. There was no love lost between him and Tammie; it was more the waste of life that hurt. Vera and Cecil had tried hard to help their last foster, but no matter what they did,

Tammie stayed on that path of destruction until it finally ran out.

"I've arranged for a cremation, but I have no place to put the ashes. Can we scatter them somewhere?"

"She liked visiting Point State Park when we were kids. I say we take her there and scatter her in the river."

"Is that legal?"

"Fuck if I know. You gonna call Morgan?"

Cam heard his brother take a long, resigned breath. "I already did. He's not interested. I'll call you back when I have more information, n'at. Yeah?"

"Sure."

The line clicked dead. Cam suddenly didn't feel like finishing the billet he had on the anvil. He powered down the shop and furnace, putting the tools away but leaving the metal to cool by itself. The drive home was uneventful. He'd already parked the bike, as the winter cold was too much this first week of January. His four-wheel drive still had trouble on the roads from the recent ice storm that made its way through the city.

Sabrina met him at the door with Rugrat firmly anchored to her shoulder. "Hey, sugar. Long day?"

"Yeah, you could say that." He entered the

mudroom and hung up his thick winter jacket before pulling off his boots. "Kyle called me."

She blinked at him over her shoulder as she made her way back into the kitchen. A big pot of something that smelled delicious bubbled away on the stove. "Really? What did he want?"

"Tammie died in Nashville. Drug overdose."

She turned from where she stirred the pot's contents. "Oh, Cam, I'm so sorry. Are you okay?"

He nodded and planted his butt against the counter in front of the stove. "Yeah, I'm good. A little numb. There's a part of me that's sad she's gone and another part of me that's glad it's over."

"I can relate. If I found out Rigo was dead, I'd be both sad and okay with it. Right now I'm pissed as hell at him for trying to sue both me and Sunstone for getting shot. Like Cicely needs to deal with that shit on top of being shot herself."

Cam picked up the matching lizard salt and pepper shakers and switched them back and forth. "I still don't understand that. It wasn't your fault. Not Cicely's either. I'm glad you don't work there anymore."

"I am, too, sugar." She yanked on a pair of oven mitts and bent over to open the appliance. The yeasty smell of fresh bread wafted over the counter. "You need to make arrangements or something?"

"Kyle is handling it." His eyes drifted over the golden crust of a round sourdough. "Did Rodrigo ever get the rest of his shit settled with Rosa?"

Sabrina rolled her eyes. "As far as I know he did. Rigo gets half of Dad's estate, and I get the other half. It's not enough to make anyone rich, but it's a good start to saving up for my own future massage practice."

He smiled. "Guess that means you're gonna stick it out here, with me."

Sabrina pulled two large bowls from the cupboard. "Was there ever any doubt? Yes, sugar. I'm sticking it out here."

Cam watched her ladle the Irish stew into the bowls and break off big chunks of bread to add to the side plates. He lifted the saltshaker with its curling lizard tail and placed it in front of her. "How 'bout we make it official?"

Dangling from the end of the tail was a ring of Damascus steel. Sabrina stared at it. "Did you make that?" Her voice quavered.

He picked it up and held it to the light to show all the colored layers. "It's not a diamond, but it's made with lots of love and care. You can call it an engagement band if you want. We can rename it later as your wedding band, or I can make a different one for that."

She slipped the ring onto her finger. "It's perfect."

Cam took her hands in his. Nervousness made his stomach feel like Jell-O, but he pressed on. "I spent a lot of time alone in my life. There was a brief moment of family, but then it was gone when Vera and Cecil passed. My brothers and I aren't close. I found the Knights, but they're still a dysfunctional mess. I never realized how much I need that in my life, something solid and steady. Some*one*." He raised her hands and kissed the spot where his ring sat on her finger. "I love you, Sabrina. I need you. I need you to be my family. Will you take me and forge a new life with me?"

Sabrina didn't make him work for it. With a wide smile, she nodded. "Yes. Of course I will."

END

OTHER BOOKS BY ML NYSTROM

IRON CITY KNIGHTS

Iron City Showdown (Free Prequel Short)

Ignite | Forge

DRAGON RUNNERS MC

Mute | Stud | Blue | Table | Brick | Dodge | Weatherman

MACATEER BROTHERS

Run With It | Ready For It | Hold It Close | Risk It All | Give It To Me

THE DUTCHMEN MC

The Price of Redemption | The Price of Forgiveness | The Price of Peace | The Price of Atonement

ACKNOWLEDGMENTS

I put words on paper every day. Sometimes just a few, and sometimes I get in the zone and it just pours out. This book was a challenge in that the storyline wove in and out of some real events and real people. I needed a female character, and Stephanie, my massage therapist, was perfect. Yes, she's the one who told me to relax my sphincter the first time she worked on me.

I also included Amanda, a surprise stepsister. Somewhere around age forty-something, she discovered she was indeed my stepdad's daughter. What a story! She's also one of the strongest, kindest, hardest-working women out there. Papa D has since passed on, but Amanda is still in touch with us, and we get to visit from time to time when we're in the same state.

Big shout-out to my editor, Kristin Scearce. She puts up with me texting her that I've hit another wall and I need her to talk me through it. Then we spend a half hour on the phone hashing through some different scenes until we find the right one.

Major thanks to my beta Brittany Shore. She has iguanas named Reptar and Rugrat. I made them beardies because of space. Another big thanks to Mandy Pederick, Kim Deister, and Andi Altvater for reading and catching all those details I missed. You have no idea how much I rely on having other eyes check behind me.

As always, I have to give a bow to the crew at Hot Tree Publishing for their support over the last eight years or so. From the first time when I held my breath and hit Send, they've been a great support and resource for me. Y'all rock!

ML Nystrom

ABOUT THE AUTHOR

ML Nystrom has had stories in her head since she was a child. All sorts of stories of fantasy, romance, mystery, and anything else that captured her interest. A voracious reader, she's spent many hours devouring books; therefore, she found it only fitting she should write a few herself!

ML has spent most of her life as a performing musician and band instrument repair technician, but that doesn't mean she's pigeonholed into one mold. She's been a university professor, belly dancer, craftsperson, soap maker, singer, rock band artist, jewelry maker, lifeguard, swim coach, and whatever else she felt like exploring. As one of her students said to her once, "Life's too short to ignore the opportunities." She has no intention of ever stopping... so welcome to her story world. She hopes you enjoy it!

JOIN MY NEWSLETTER:
WWW.MLNYSTROM.COM/CONTACT

facebook.com/authorMLNystrom

instagram.com/mlnystrom

bookbub.com/authors/ml-nystrom

ABOUT THE PUBLISHER

Hot Tree Publishing loves love. Publishing adult romantic fiction, HTPubs are all about diverse reads featuring heroes and heroines to swoon over. Since opening in 2015, HTPubs have published more than 350 titles across the wide and diverse range of romantic genres. If you're chasing a happily ever after in your favourite subgenre, HTPubs have you covered.

Interested in discovering more amazing reads brought to you by Hot Tree Publishing? Head over to the website for information:

WWW.HOTTREEPUBLISHING.COM

facebook.com/hottreepublishing
instagram.com/hottreepublishing
tiktok.com/@hottreepublishing

www.ingramcontent.com/pod-product-compliance
Lightning Source LLC
LaVergne TN
LVHW050028080526
838202LV00070B/6963